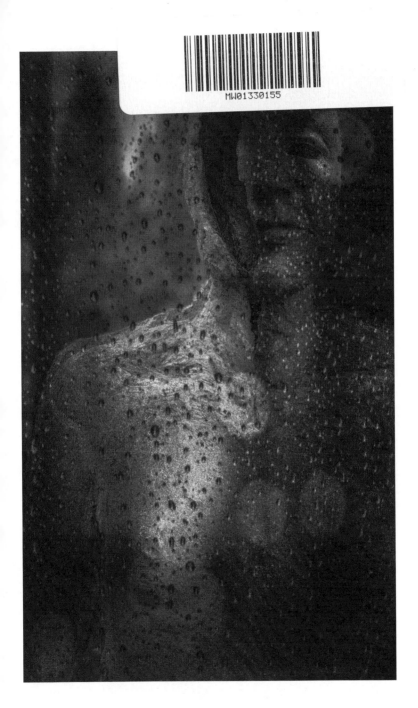

Dreams of a Cosmicist

Dreams of a Cosmicist is © 2020 Abdul Nakra. All Rights Reserved. No part of this book may be used or reproduced in any manner whatsoever, including Internet usage, without written permission from Abdul Nakra, except in the case of brief quotations embodied in critical articles and reviews.

Dedicated to the nihilists, cosmic pessimists and misanthropes of the world who face existence with raw honesty. Your presence makes me feel less alone in this world, although that feeling is, as we both know, nothing more than a comfortable illusion.

Table of Contents

1 - Foreword

Anti-Cosmic Electrical Resistance

7 - The A'akbishan Women
18 - The Ring of Apothul
28 - The Carnivorous Plants of Ulba'ak
36 - The Grey Hat Sect
61 - The Trial of Frater Mark
69 - The Hyperborean Isle of Rashuth

Meanderings of a Wicked Soul

89 - The Green Harlequin
116 - The Star
127 - Euthanasia
141 - The Hunger
151 - The Cities are Burning

Foreword

If there is one thing I dislike very much (and who am I kidding, there are many things I dislike very much) it is a foreword that is too long. But at least a foreword is generally written by the author themselves. Introductions written by a person who is not the author are horrendous things intended to color the perspective of the work that follows for the would-be-reader. That a person should consider their outside perspective as valid enough to be forced onto the perspective of others is perhaps the pinnacle of absurdity, and is a reflection of much of what is wrong with this world.

The reader must determine for themselves what the meaning of a work of literature is. It is not for anyone to attempt to determine this for them. Having written the contents of the present work I still do not believe it to be my place to attempt to color your vision of it.

What these stories mean to you, if anything at all, will be both subjective and illusory.

What I will elaborate upon however is some of the background in my writing these works. The collection of stories which I have entitled *Anti-Cosmic Electrical Resistance* were written in 2015 and were originally intended to be included in the works of a collective of individuals that I was then associated with. The problem was, naturally, that I was the only person who was willing to do the work of writing, so that project was shelved and these stories have not seen the light of day until the present time. I had all but forgotten about them until, more recently, I began to write short fictional stories again, following a period of years in which I have been preoccupied with other activities.

As such, I have decided to make the present work a body of two collections of stories. The first, as I have mentioned, were written several years ago. The second collection, *Meanderings of a Wicked Soul*, was written much more recently; with the exception of *The Cities are Burning*, which was written in 2019, the remainder were written in the first week of January, 2020, although conceptions for some of them began in 2019.

So much for the phenomenon of the foreword. I have nothing left to say to you.

Anti-Cosmic Electrical Resistance

The A'akbishan Women

It is perhaps far too often that the human, with their limited spectrum of analysis, will seek to explore the depths of unknown expanse without first having thoroughly explored the known. Too often also has man been drawn lustfully by the siren's song, only to crash upon the rocky shore of the illusions they have weaved. I write this work as a testament to my own experiences in the exploration of the unknown, particularly pertaining to certain forbidden realms of which far too many speak lightly in our modern time. At this time of writing I am bedridden and exercising every bit of my will power to remain in a lucid and waking state, for the siren's song is even now calling me to return to them.

My birth was of such an alignment as to allow for

a natural tendency towards dreaming, whether by night or day. As a child and even now into my young adulthood I have dreamt of fantastic things; worlds entirely functioning and as real as any that you or I may know of in our world. The nature of my dreams have changed throughout my progression of years and many lands once visited are now but a pleasantly reminiscent memory of a different place and time. It is all too easy to become lost in the world of dreams and that world has inspired many amongst us towards creative expression during our waking life, effectively transmitting the imagined into the tangible. I must confess that at an early age I had become so fascinated by the world of dreams as to pay little mind to worldly dynamics, and as such have always been a loner.

While many worlds that I have explored in my dreams have been fantastic and beautiful, their equal opposite has also appeared frequently in the form of desolate and terrible lands. So too do the inhabitants of either type of world reflect their environments. The darker worlds, though terrible, initially attracted me due to the curious phenomena that they allow; namely lucidity of the dreaming experiences. Perhaps I gave myself too much to these darker worlds and beings, but in exchange was granted a freedom that no waking phenomenon could ever grant me. In time and from a fairly young age I was able to lucidly navigate the dream worlds to the degree that in my waking life I had crafted maps, detailing entry points, cities, natural areas and the like.

It was around my fourteenth year of life that I began to dream of the spiders. I had at that time been horribly arachnophobic, a fear long since surpassed but once very real to me. The dreams started in familiar places such as the basement of my then home wherein I would start up the stairs but become overwhelmed by countless myriads of black spiders, unable to escape them and ultimately waking up in terror. This dream was recurring, occasionally changing so that the spiders would emerge from out of the mouth and orifices of a family member in a similar manner as previously described. As horrifying as these visions were, I found them intriguing and accordingly found myself drawing spiders frequently while awake. While I was in school rather than learning I would be drawing spiders, or even better would be drifting into a hypnogogic trance that allowed me to enter the dream worlds. The dreams soon began to take on a more complex nature. Often time I would be amidst suburban neighborhoods walking or exploring, only to observe larger than human size spiders devouring humans on the streets. At times during these visions I would be hiding inside of a house, observing from the window. At this time the fears began to subside slightly, as though the spider in its larger form was less frightening in its symbolism than a myriad in their minute form. Was it simply the overwhelming numbers of them that frightened me at that time? I am not sure and may never know, for time is short and its web is vast.

These dreams persisted continuously and I in time realized their nature to be of a particular region of alternative reality wherein such large arachnids lived alongside humans as a competitor for apex-predation. At the age of sixteen I befriended the son of a priest of Lucumi who was very knowledgeable in matters of alternative dimensions and the races that reside there. I would occasionally discuss my dream experiences with him and in the instance of the large spiders he informed me of a race called the Wiha'a, large spiders with humanoid heads that were known of in the Lucumi tradition to feed off of human infants. The priest had claimed to have seen one near a river as a child and stated that they always utilized water or moisture as a means to enter this world, as many spirits or other-dimensional beings did, and would come to this world not only to feed but also to sleep, as seconds of time in our world were equal to many hours' worth in theirs. He himself was disgusted and frightened by these beings but the large spiders remained to me a source of fascination and I never did heed his warnings concerning them. The fear was still strong at this point in my life and yet even fear was to me a reservoir of vast power worthy of my ambitious pursuit to discover the means of its apprehension, leading to a more complete mastery over my dream explorations and a general mastery of self.

It was also around that time in my life that large spiders would appear quite frequently around me, and though terrified I began to take greater notice of their behaviors. For example I noticed that spiders always travel in pairs of two, and though they appear as loners they in truth form web-like networks amongst themselves, collectively and cunningly covering a territory with webs so as to allow for an even distribution of food. As time went on it became apparent that my fear of spiders was foolish, for these beings were likely far more frightened of me than I of them, and yet despite this some invisible influence persisted in sending them to me.

On a night several weeks ago I entered the dream state and arrived at the familiar house that I had now been utilizing as my gateway into the suburban region called Lengon Hills. As per usual I looked through the window prior to leaving, as the large spiders were often outside at any given time and I made it a habit to avoid leaving the house when they were outside. The inhabitants of this house had been devoured some time ago yet the house remained in excellent shape, likely the result of a much slower rate of entropy on this plane. Seeing that the street was empty, I emerged from the house. Tonight I was to venture into the Lengon Forest, a place few of its human inhabitants ever desired to enter for despite its beauty it was known to be a home to the spiders, which the local people said were ruled by a group of beings called the A'akbish. The forest was several blocks from my point of entry but I encountered no person or spider on my walk to it. It was a beautiful dawn in this world and by now I knew it would likely remain dawn for the entirety of my stay here. Stars were still visible in the sky above at this time and the moon in its disseminating phase hung high so as to cast an extra glow upon the streets, contrasting the first blue and violet hues that informed of the sun in its rising. As I approached the forest the black and grey concrete streets were exchanged for a grand display of green.

I entered the forest and soon came upon a stream that I would follow for some time, enjoying the gentle sound of the running water that contrasted so nicely the rare and otherworldy songs of birds above me that few will ever hear. I often enjoyed walks like these in this world and my initial exploration of the forest was met positively. Once or twice I observed the large spiders in the distance, and more than a few times did I observe large clusters of webs that towered over my height, but keeping my distance I was thus far safe. I returned to my entry point after some time and departed for my waking life though would return to this place again later that night for further exploration.

Upon my re-entry to the Lengon Hills that night I observed one of the spiders towards the corner of the block of entry and after waiting a few moments decided I would leave and take a detour to the forest. Once in the forest I followed the same stream as during the previous night and began to formulate a more detailed mental map of the forest area. I walked much farther than the previous night and eventually came upon a white house whose architectural style was unrecognizable but of which was astoundingly beautiful. To compare it with St. Basil's cathedral would not do its beauty any justice but would provide something of an architectural comparison, and yet in comparative scale of size it was minute in stature. I felt inclined to view it more closely and proceeded further on towards it and there was not a rustle out of place in the forest as I did so, for I payed close attention to my surroundings lest one of the spiders or another such being ambush its unsuspecting prey.

As I reached the perimeter of the house I put out my hand to touch its wall, for it appeared to be of a substance I could not quite identify. It felt soft and silky yet firm enough to stand on its own, and upon touching it there appeared a subtle wave of magnetism that reverberated throughout the structure from the point of impact and thence returned to that point. It was not unusual in my dream explorations to encounter strange and unusual manifestations of matter but I had never before encountered anything resembling this type. A sudden rustling of underbrush drew my attention and weariness and a short moment later I observed an exceptionally beautiful woman walk out from around the other side of the house. She was a light skinned brunette with green eyes and upon seeing me there was a brief moment of what looked like surprise in her eyes, and then a welcoming smile. I returned the smile and greeted her, to which she returned an inviting gesture towards her and turned around to walk. I followed her automatically, in retrospect feeling almost hypnotized by her beauty. Around the other side of the circular perimeter of the house was a tall open doorway through which she beckoned me to enter, and she followed me in as I did so. Inside the house was comprised of a fantastic woodworking rivaled only by the most illustrious master craftsmen of our world, however upon closer inspection I saw that it was not wood at all but a more condensed form of the silky outer material. I was guided by the woman into what seemed to be a sitting room and sat beside her on a type of couch. She examined me deeply as though reading into the memories and desires of my soul, then stood and walked over to a window where, looking somewhat saddened, she began to sing. The tones that she emitted were marvelously elegant and of a manner only found in a world such as that one, with each melody touching and moving my heart and soul with longing, first for something ineffable and beyond my conception but gradually this desire became coagulated into a desire for the very woman whose voice gently serenaded me in a language whose dialect I did not comprehend rationally and yet intuitively understood it greater than any language that I logically apprehended.

Her eyes turned from the window and met mine while she blushed gently, and I instinctively arose to meet her with a kiss. Some while later two more alluring women entered the room, each carrying a similar appearance and aura as the first though each of them having slightly differing features, and none more beautiful than the other. Without words we communicated as though by subtle fibers connecting our hearts and minds. By this means we shared the deepest qualities of ourselves through subtly intense emotions and intuitions. I began to see that there were subtle difference between the three women and that wherever one had an absence of some quality the others supplemented what was required for equilibrium. The three nameless women brought me upstairs and showed me a room containing a curious mirror whose reflection appeared mercurial and whose border was like that of obsidian. I understood that this was to be an entry-point through which I may return at any time to their home in this world where I would be a welcomed and beloved guest. I must admit that I did not want to leave, feeling as though I had my three fates woven for me at this place, but from that night until today I did return to that world each night and only ever through the portal at that strange house.

As time went on I developed a deeper relationship with these three women, both individually and with them collectively. Though it has only been a few weeks, and exactly how many I have lost count, it quickly felt as though I had been intoxicated by their embrace for aeons. I began to feel a sense of suffering and longing not unlike that which the first unnamed woman expressed melodiously during our first meeting whenever away from them, and as such had retreated even further from the world in order to remain in the dark confines of my home where I could sleep as much as humanly possible to be with them.

It was during one of the most recent nights that an unusual event occurred. I may have caught them off-guard, perhaps because my own essence was becoming affixed to the environment of the house, but upon entering their home on that day I perceived something quite disturbing. I had entered as always through the mirror and walked over to the ledge that overlooked the lower floor and their equivalent of a kitchen. What

I saw sent a wave of terror and surprise through me, for there were the three of them plus one other sitting in the room in the form of large spiders. They noticed me immediately and kindly beckoned me down to them, and when I turned from them and looked again they were as alluring as ever. I descended the stairs to them and sat at a table facing the three of them; the fourth that I had apparently seen was nowhere to be found. I was aware of a strange aura about the room and a subtle pinkish-violet light. I was disturbed at what I had seen and began to contemplate mentally whether or not I had simply allowed myself to have been influenced by the superstitions of the people from the Lengon Hills suburb, so that my vision had been distorted by my own shadow. The three of them gazed at me and I noticed that the features of their faces were changing gradually, always in such a fashion as that which would be more beautiful to my personal perception. Upon this observation I realized that I had been lulled into an allurement of their devise and felt disturbed by the notion. They however spared no expense at my comfort and at continuing their method of allurement, and I must confess to having chosen to believe in their illusion despite having seen the horrible truth beneath it.

The motivations behind the actions of these women was however still a mystery to me in the proceeding days and any thought in which I considered not to return to that place was met only with fear and sadness, for I had fallen in love with my predators. It was around this time that while awake I had developed a stronger second sight and what I saw only accumulated upon my fear and confusion, for there were arranged around my room what appeared to be clustered egg sacks. With each passing day these clusters appeared ever more volatile and the behavior of the women had changed as well, for they now insisted that I would consume a type of blackish fluid at any time I had entered their home. Coincidentally I became bed-ridden and have been forced to sleep if only to escape the pain that feels as though my insides are burning, though even with the pain I still have the insatiable desire to return to my beloved.

I will conclude this paper here for I have become weak and the reliving of this experience has drained much from me; perhaps there is more than that which is draining me, for I question from what source these eggs will receive their nourishment and as I gaze at them now it appears that the first signs of their hatching are occurring.

The Ring of Apothul

Long have I been the seeker of knowledge and wisdom in any form capable of releasing me from the quarantined boundaries of this mundane sphere of earthly matter. Through my intensive and devotional study of the occult sciences I have accomplished much upon the inner planes of my being, and upon the outer planes I have the freedom that I earnestly seek. I began to live the life of a travelling nomad some years ago and began to drift around the earth, moving wherever the currents would compel my intuitions and accordingly seeing a vast expanse of the earth. Through my travels I have under most circumstances remained in solitude, with the occasional exception being found in the Magickal initiations that I received in such diverse regions as West Africa, Brazil, Albania, and New Zealand.

At the time that the following events occurred I was travelling throughout Europe in search of certain rare occult manuscripts published by notoriously dangerous Magickal orders located in Northern Europe. Whilst in Denmark where I had been enjoying some of the local flavors of the Red Light District of the Netherlands I came upon an unusual high end esoteric bookstore. As I entered the store the man behind the register raised his eyes above the dark leather tome in front of him with an unpleasant glare, which I returned, and I proceeded to explore the contents of the small red shop. The shelves were lined with neatly arranged leather and cloth bound texts, many or perhaps most of them pertaining to the darker arts.

As I scanned the many titles rapidly many caught my interest but my eyes soon rested upon a particular text I had been seeking, Liber Shoqath, written by the Temple of the Black Flame. It was bound in what appeared to be the skin of some type of slightly bluish amphibian, and when I later asked the shopkeeper he himself was not aware of what it was exactly but called it an "exotic flesh". Glancing through its contents I saw that it did not disappoint its reputation, nor my expectation. I purchased it for a steep price, well worth it considering its rarity, and was left with enough money for my hostel stay following some several nights.

Upon returning to the old hostel, and avoiding the temptations of the night walking women who also resided there, I entered my small room and at once set forth to the study of Liber Shoqath. Throughout the text, apart from its blackened gnosis, were instructions for the crafting of various otherworldy instruments. While I did plan on working through the entire system of gnosis that the text outlined from beginning to end, there was one element of the text that had settled firmly upon my mind; that of the Ring of Apothul. This ring was apparently only to be found in an abysmal and extraterrestrial region called Abudal, accessible by the astral plane. Upon obtaining the ring at that place it was instructed that its wielder would discover the means of transmitting its astral vibration into the material world. This would be a demonstration of the powers endowed upon its wearer and would be one ability amongst the myriad of godlike abilities it promised to bestow and of which were not seen upon earth since the Hyperborean age and which tapped an energy source even more primordial and inversely existent to any perceptible form of linearity.

I performed on that very night the initiating rituals as prescribed in the text which involved the sacrifice of blood and seminal fluids upon a sigilized image carved onto my own solar plexus, which would hereby serve as a gateway to Abudal. The rite was strong and the energy was almost overwhelming so that I found myself entering a state of sleep rather automatically. A world soon began to take form around me and I was standing at the blue-misty outskirts of an unusual city. This curious fog seemed to overwhelm the entirety of the city and though there were buildings comprised of a type of quasi-primitive architecture I was unable to perceive how tall the expanse of the larger ones was. I entered the city limits and observed my surroundings, perceiving the building structures to be comprised of a type of porous and ebony wood-like material. An unusual type of moss like substance had colonized much of the building structures of the city, casting a greenish iridescence upon the blue fog. The inhabitants of the city were large and scaly humanoid type creatures which Liber Shoqath has referred to as the Sorgalaq. Many amongst them appeared strong but there were others who seemed weak or ill.

Not losing sight of my reason for being in this place, I brought to my vision the sigil of the Ring of Apothul and held it there until I understood its location to be at that of a tall looking building in the distance. I walked through the slum-like streets until reaching this building, which did appear somewhat cleaner than many of the others thus far seen in Abudal. Through the door was a type of lobby, akin to that of an office building or hotel. The man at the front desk asked me to sign in and I did so, noting the unusual nature of the other names written on the list, one of which was clearly human like my own but all else of an extraterrestrial nature. I walked over to the old fashioned gated elevator and was taken up to the floor that I knew held the ring according to my clairvoyant vision which casted a reddish-violet glow in its direction. When the elevator arrived at the 23rd floor of the strange building I walked out into what appeared to be the hallway of a hotel with uniform doors lining either side. I started forward and as I made my way along the hallway saw that a curious type of mirror-like substance lined either side of the hall. I arrived at the burgundy colored door which read "Yg" and entered the room that is entranced.

The room itself was not quite what I had expected; though in truth with matters such as this it is better off not to have any specific expectations. Around the room were scattered stacks of papers and boxes filled with small and unusual trinkets. Various rings and other items were carelessly arranged around the room. The glow that I had been following was settled upon a black box in the corner of the room and when walking up to it I immediately recognized the ring I had been seeking. It was silver and appeared to be cast around the form of an unusually small skull. A voice from behind me said "You will want to put that on the middle finger of your dominant hand" and I turned to see a large Sorgalaq man. He introduced himself as a strange name that I didn't quite catch and then told me to call him Aphrath. He seemed to me to be of an easy-going demeanor though that may have just been the appearance he put on. He proceeded to instruct me in the basic method to the utilization of the Ring of Apothul; namely that it would enhance tremendously whatever force I would apply through it. I was never one to care for astral chatter so I thanked him and went on my way. After I had called the gated elevator up and was awaiting it I pondered to myself how I would return to the world of matter with the ring and decided I would begin to load my will power into it.

By the time I reached the misty outskirts of Abudal and gazed upon the void-like wastelands surrounding it I began my attempts to return to my world with the ring. Each attempt was futile and would at best cause me to enter a partially waking state wherein I could see that the ring had not carried forth any transference into matter. I returned fully into the astral plane, slightly frustrated but enjoying the new challenge nonetheless. I attempted to bend my will through and around this ring in a myriad of means but always failed to produce the desired result, although several other fascinating manifestations did occur including what appeared to be the opening of an
octagon of gateways around myself, leading to realms I would not yet enter but which appeared to me reminiscent of the Quuthian tunnels of Shutath.

I decided to return to the location at which I had discovered the ring, believing that the Sorgalaq man Aphrath may have had information that could assist me. I returned the way that I came, having to sign in again to at the front desk of the building, and upon entering the room titled Yg found a very different atmosphere. Rather than the cluttered mess of a hotel room I had visited previously, I now stood in a luxurious room arranged like an office. I took note of the strange leathers that covered the chairs which were similar to that upon which Liber Shoqath was bound. Aphrath was sitting at a large ebony desk and smoking a peculiar type of cigarette of the type which he offered to me. As I inhaled the strange blue smoke I felt an immense feeling of calm come upon me and he asked why I had returned after taking the ring. I informed him of my dilemma of returning to my own world with the ring and he made a proposition to me that in exchange for running some local errands for him he would teach me what I sought to know. I agreed to his proposition, seeing no reason to turn away at this point. He told me to relax and smoke the strange cigarette for awhile but, sensing that I was somewhat pressed for time, shrugged his shoulders and produced several small bags filled with a blue paste. He informed me that these were called Nabtung, a type of recreational intoxicant that the cigarette I smoked had apparently been dusted with. Each bag had a location clairvoyantly placed upon it that would direct me to the intended destination where they were to be delivered.

I left to make the local deliveries of nabtung and soon understood why Abudal had such a slum-like feel to it, as it was very overrun with drug use. I thought to myself that it was looking like a dirtier otherworldy version of the Netherlands all the time, and the correspondences between finding Liber Shoqath there and venturing here interested me. This pattern of returning to the hotel and leaving to deliver packets of nabtung was recurring for awhile and I had yet to learn a thing concerning the transference of the ring. I had inquired about this with Aphrath but he insisted that it was a busy day and I would have to keep working. One my fourth return trip I became frustrated and made what was perhaps a mistake of threatening Aphrath by force, to which he responded by simply frowning and projecting a pulse from his mind's eye into my own which rendered me unconscious.

When I awoke I was in a strange open room with other humans. They welcomed me with a mixture of sadness and frustration, informing me that there was no way to escape this floor of the building. Not one amongst us recalled how we became entrapped there. By the appearance of some of the other humans it appeared that they had been there for some time; their faces were gaunt and I wondered if their physical bodies were now kept in a comatose state permanently. At the thought of this I pondered how such a relation between the astral and physical plane could influence my transmitting the ring into matter, and it was then that I noticed the ring to no longer be present upon my hand. I admit that a slight sense of claustrophobia fell over me at this point; perhaps I let my psychic guard down and became overly receptive to the feelings of the prisoners around me. For some time I contemplated a way out of this particular floor of the building but there were no doors, windows, or loose panels of any kind. Instead all that was here were a wall of toilets, a crudely laid tile floor, and a mirrored wall on one side of the large room that gave an appearance of the room being larger than it was. I stared at this mirror for awhile and suddenly an idea came to me. I walked over to the mirror and envisioned myself holding the Black Wass Scepter of Shutath and concentrated this image until the scepter was in my hand on my side of the reflection. Now that I had this scepter in hand, which I had learned about in a dream excursion long ago, I passed through the mirror as though it were a barrier of water.

On the other side of the mirror portal that I had opened I found myself standing once again at the edge of Abudal. I had no intention now of returning to Abudal yet still desired the ring of Apothul. Locating it remotely, where I saw it was once again in a small box of assorted items likely awaiting the next human to seek it; I utilized the powers of the Wass scepter to relocate the ring to my present location, and placing it on my hand, reopened the octagonal tunnels as I had earlier opened. The eight portals around me offered passages into various worlds of differing physics and I was looking in particular for one that touched closely upon the etheric planes while existing in a physically denser nature of physics. I decide quickly upon the tunnel called Qu'ulelfi and at the moment of my decision the environment around me becomes a magenta colored hue that saturates all that is within my vision. A moment later, after what feels like having been squeezed through a pipe, the magenta light fades but does not disappear completely and I find myself in a dark swamp.

The magenta hued mist is thick but through it I can see the inverted horned moon in the sky above. Around me splash strange creatures that I cannot quite catch an accurate glimpse of, while within the mists myriadic forms assemble and disassemble spontaneously, cascading through the air. Knowing that being knee deep in the swamp of this plane is probably unsafe I seek dry land, with no avail. The heaviness of this world weighed on me heavily and I began to notice both the scepter and ring undergoing a rapid decay rate, for the excelled rate of entropy found in this world was a forgotten variable upon my entrance into it. I attempted to open the octagram of portals but the light rapidly decayed inversely, making my escape through the portals impossible and as the myriadic misty forms continued to coagulate around me I realized that I would have to depart from this world quickly. It was then that I departed from the astral plane, leaving behind both the scepter and ring, my experiment failed and my physical body sick for about a week of time after that.

I am not sure what became of the ring of Apothul; perhaps it returned to the little box where it was carelessly tossed in that building in Abudal, or perhaps it remains in the swamplands of Qu'ulelfi. I have not since gone back to look for it and I do not believe I will, for the gnosis obtained through the experience of its obtainment and loss was in itself the prize that I brought back from my journey and which endures with me to this day, though the illness that resulted from those experiences has also never entirely been purged from my body.

The Carnivorous Plants of Ulba'ak

Dr. Salvador Basurto was an ambitious young scientist who, having recently completed his doctorate schooling in the field of ethnobotany, desired immediately to begin the work that would allow him to make his impact upon the scientific community. However, he soon found out after his graduation from the University of Barcelona that between required internships and research experience it would be a difficult task to immediately set forth into his desired research project. It was no surprise then that, given the opportunity several years later to receive private funding for research from a family patron, Dr. Basurto jumped at the opportunity to fulfill his aspirations.

The nature of his research was inspired, rather peculiarly for a man of science, by a pseudo-scientific book he came upon during his years in high school entitled The Lost Continent and its Descendants. This book described an ancient continent commonly known as Lemuria which existed at one time in the South-Pacific Ocean. It was stated in the book that at the time of and prior to the destruction of Lemuria, certain amongst its inhabitants departed for nearby islands, while others were geographically placed so as to be broadly unaffected by the catastrophe that destroyed the remainder of the island. These beings were stated to have de-evolved somewhat from their once nearly superhuman state into the Pacific Islander humans by mixing with early Neanderthals and homo-sapiens. In time tribes of these humans migrated to South America where they established small societies and cults akin to the ancient systems and culture that generated them. Rumor had it, according to the book, that the people of Lemuria and their descendants excelled at cultivating marvelous and rare geneses of plants which could presently be located within deep uncharted regions of the Brazilian Amazon rainforest. This book made quite an impact upon Dr. Basurto and was an early inspiration for his future choice of profession.

It was a very hot spring day when Dr. Basurto arrived at the airport at Bon Vista and as he awaited his transfer flight to Manaus he noted to himself the remarkable change in seasons, for in his native Spain the year was waning towards autumn while in Brazil the year was just now ascending towards its zenith of summer. His transfer flight followed soon and upon arriving at the Manaus airport was met by his guide, a fluently Spanish-speaking Brazilian man named Lucas, who was to take him by boat along the Amazon River as far as the Jarua. Anxious to begin his research, they embarked immediately.

The journey along the river was long and hot though Dr. Basurto marveled at the rich expanse of biological diversity. As they travelled along the muddy brown river there was intense greens of nearly every conceivable shade within view, and the sounds of a myriad of life forms for its company. At night the two men would stop at a river bank to camp, and Dr. Basurto could not resist asking his guide Lucas about the tribes he had read about, to which Lucas simply shrugged and said that there were many strange rumors told to him as a child about tribes such as those but he had never seen them.

The journey lasted four days and on the fifth they had at last reached the Jarua river. Dr. Basurto and Lucas bid each other farewell until Lucas' return trip to this location in two weeks to come, and the meeting area was marked by a large orange banner. Dr. Basurto watched for a moment as Lucas maneuvered the boat to return to Manaus and proceeded to enter the rainforest. He had requested two weeks worth of non- perishable food provisions in his pack and was fairly knowledgeable of edible plants if necessary to consume them. He walked southwest and after several hours came upon his first discovery.

The fungi were unlike any he had studied nor to his knowledge that had been yet discovered. Their milky texture colored in an unusual violet and orange seemed almost to glow even in the daylight, while it's lower part displayed whitish-red gills from which countless spores doubtlessly emerged. Several samples were collected and the name Psilocybin Yuggothensis was decided upon for the genus. It was an exciting moment for the doctor for he had not only made his first pioneering discovery, but had stumbled upon an indication that the rumors of his adolescent obsession could in fact be true.

The next two hours or so were without particular significance, save for the increase in density of that particular fungi, and then it was though he had stumbled into a new world.

The extensive variety of colors stimulates his olfactory senses like nothing ever had, and with careful analysis he determined that there was in fact an array of undiscovered carnivorous plant species present. He began to take samples but the variety only continued to increase and when he had counted over thirty unique and undiscovered species he decided to continue walking so as to find a space in which to set up his mosquito net hammock. As he began to tie the hammock to two trees he heard a curious sound and peering through the trees observed a child, or perhaps it was a very small man, picking leaves from a bush. The person was speaking a strange language not at all resembling any amongst the indigenous Amazon tribal languages Dr. Basurto had studied. This was his opportunity to confirm the rumors of his book concerning the Ta'ake-wanu tribe and, placing aside the strange restless exhaustion that befell him, he approached the indigenous person.

As he approached him, the wild haired boy turned to the doctor and with a strangely dark smile nodded and continued to speak the language as before. As the boy walked away the doctor followed him, leaving his equipment behind, and after twenty minutes or so found himself standing at the edge of a native village. The village was perhaps less primitive than many others in the Amazon basin, for it displayed an archaic stone working which was albeit overgrown with unusual vined plants that appeared to move with a sort of melodic rhythm that seemed somehow alien to the natural rhythm of the rainforest as he had known it several hours earlier.

Several amongst the villagers had taken notice of the doctor and two men, an elder and curandero it was assumed, approached the doctor. They eyed him curiously and the curandero sent a young boy away, who returned a moment later holding a crude stone container filled with a milky liquid. This, the curandero offered to Dr. Basurto who accepted kindly this gift of welcome as he had read was common amongst many indigenous peoples. He regretted that he had no gift to offer in exchange but this appeared of no matter to the curandero who ushered him into a nearby dwelling hut.

The hut was decorated with plants unlike Dr. Basurto had ever perceived, as were those that surrounded the entirety of the village, and like the strange vines they all appeared to move as though dancing to some otherworldly hypnosis. Markings of an alphabet resembling none known to modern man was etched upon the inner walls and the doctor regretted not having brought with him his sketching book from the campsite. At the thought of the campsite there was a stir of anxiety in his gut, for it was becoming night now and he was in truth unsure of which direction he had entered the village from; he thought to himself that he must have become over excited at the prospect of his discoveries, for he felt strangely overheated and restless. Reaching for his canteen he saw that this too had been left behind and he motioned for water to the curandero who instead handed him a basin filled with a brown fluid. Dr. Basurto drank the brown fluid quickly and then unexpectedly drifted into a state of unconsciousness.

When he awoke he was on a mat in the curandero's tent and felt a terrible sense of dehydration, yet it did not seem that obtaining water here would be an easy task. The curandero however, seeing that he had awoken, brought to him a container of water which he drank in its entirety. It was then that he noticed the peculiar tattoos that covered the curandero in near entirety and which appeared to fluctuate to a similar hypnotic movement as that of the strange plants of this place. Standing and walking outside, he saw that the entirety of the village appeared to be decorated in this manner.

They appeared to be in preparation of a ceremony for they held torches, wore paint and were gathered in the village center despite the time of night, though for all he knew this may have been a daily custom to them.

The curandero motioned for him to follow and they embarked away from the remainder of the village and into the jungle. Perhaps he had discovered the location of his supplies Dr Basurto thought. In a short while, which seemed in length much longer than it was, they were standing at the mouth of a vast pit that seemed out of place in the otherwise lush and dense forest. Dr Basurto sensed that something unusual was occurring yet felt powerless to inquire of it. A movement in the pit below cut through his thoughts and he saw first a yellow and pink glow of lights which became increasingly bright and massive in size. A moment later the contents of the pit was revealed as an enormous carnivorous plant resembling a Nepenthes. Its massive breadth was many times his size and he heard the curandero, or perhaps this was one of the dark brujos he had been warned about, chanting a word Huataqu repeatedly. Dr Brasuro suddenly became horrified at the prospect of what may have come lest he depart immediately and, pushing the curandero onto the ground, he ran into the night frantically hoping that he would not cross the village once again. At a point when he was forced to stop and rest a moment, seeking any source of hydration around him, he spotted what he believed was a citrus fruit but in fact was a Brazilian pepper berry that caused a severe rash in his esophagus.

Amidst his frantic running and gasping for breath; an hour or so later no less, he stumbled upon a stone and crashed to the ground, splitting his skull upon a rock which a later autopsy revealed was fatal. He was found four weeks later by a search party after having not met Lucas at the orange banner and his campsite was discovered, curiously, to be several days' journey on foot from his location.

The autopsy noted, also curiously, that it appeared he had ingested an exceedingly heavy dose of rare fungi spores from the air which contained hallucinogenic chemical compounds as yet undiscovered by modern science and it was determined that in a fit of hallucinating delirium he must have lost awareness of himself and absentmindedly fell to his death. The pathologist, himself having an interest in flora and fauna, proceeded to share his new discovery with the scientific community where it eventually received high acclaim, for many stated that its effects allowed for a direct experience of the divine that temporarily released one from the limiting boundaries of the world of matter.

The Grey Hat Sect

December 11th, 1989 - Noon

I arrived in Kathmandu, Nepal just a few hours earlier and am presently enjoying a large plate of momo dumplings as I write in a small restaurant. Kathmandu is such a mess! Not what I had expected at all, though with so many American tourists it is not surprising. The once pristine Bagmati river is now filled with polluted debris and the streets are scarcely any different. But all complaints aside, the city is alive with excitement and I suppose is fulfilling its place as a transition point well enough. I've brought my own sleeping bag and tent, which are guaranteed to withstand temperatures below freezing, and only intend to pick up a few items from the market unless anything special catches my eye. The prices for the trekking permits in the north-eastern region where I intend to venture were outrageous and permits for Mustang are even worse so I purchased a more limited trekking permit and will commence as intended regardless, though will have to avoid the main roads and any patrolmen. This may set me back a few days overall but if the main trails are as full of tourists as Kathmandu it will be a much welcomed isolation. I had already exchanged a good portion of my money into Nepalese currency to be utilized at various villages along the trekking routes but am not sure if I will now have the opportunity, no matter though. The momo is excellent by the way; I will have to find out what this aromatic dipping sauce is. There is nothing quite like the spicy scents of South-East Asian spices. The air here is filled with saffron, turmeric and various other spices that I could not name offhand.

Note that the dipping sauce is tomato chutney; the waiter was pleased to tell me.

Later that Evening
I'm at the hostel now; I elected for a small private room rather than a bunkmate. Picked up enough preserved meat to last me two weeks or so, a large water canteen that can be refilled frequently at the many rivers that frequent the valleys I'll be trekking, and a beautiful old knife with a bone handle. The merchant told me it belonged to an old monk, though my senses haven't determined yet whether or not this is true. In any case it may be useful and despite its age is in excellent shape and bears a sharp crescent shaped blade. I also purchased clothing like the Sherpas wear in the winter so as to appear inconspicuous and a heavy coat of ox

wool. The market in general was filled with wares made from nearby villages and monasteries and I see that the people here have been successfully enterprising upon the growing tourist industry that the Himalayas have attracted to Westerners throughout this past century. It doesn't seem to be in any state of decline and I am happy to have come when I did and not later for it seems that the isolated roof of the world is becoming ever more populous. If all goes well I will reside here in an area far removed from all of this however. I had best get an early sleep for tomorrow morning I'll be departing eastward early.

December 12th - Evening
Incredible how many tourist trekkers were out on the trails, it was far worse than I had expected. I am genuinely surprised to see so many people here in the winter, but I suppose to the Sherpas and others who live here all year are also travelling the trails so why not trekkers. In any case I have had to wander far off the trail to the north which in all likelihood works out well since I had planned on cutting steadily towards the north east. By now it will be almost entirely eastward following the direction of the rising sun. Speaking of the sun, it is setting as I write and the scenery atop this quiet hillside is outstanding. There is snow as far as I can see, for apparently the winter arrived early this year. I may not have many nights to camp on such a high plane of land if I am to remain unnoticed and may already be nearing the area outside of my permitted range, but I am certainly enjoying it tonight. I'm thankful that I broke in my boots before this

journey otherwise my feet might be in a lot of pain and with so much farther to walk. Though with no definite destination who knows, perhaps I will chance upon a wandering shaman who can initiate me into the practices of Bon amidst the great white expanse of mountains and snow. Until then I shall march east!

December 13th – Morning
It is twilight now and the sun is just creeping above the horizon in a display of deep red that pierces the cloudy dark sky. I am not writing to describe the beauty of the scenery however, and instead have had a remarkable dream that I wish to transcribe in as great a detail as possible.

I was walking along a high mountain pass when spontaneously there appeared an array of dancing Dakinis in their wrathful manifestations. The tiger, serpent, and ox headed women of many colors danced naked and sang beautiful songs in their own languages. I realized that I too was naked and danced with them for a time. At a point, and with no prior notice, their wrathful nature became dominant and I was torn to pieces by them yet retained my conscious awareness. A great cauldron that seemed to be of a bronze and iron alloy appeared over a searing flame and the components of my body were ripped into smaller parts and tossed into the cauldron of boiling liquid like a soup. The Dakinis danced around the cauldron for some time, singing a different and somewhat more ominous song, as the water became denser and my components formed a sort of stew. When the stew had finished, and by now I had become at wholly at one with it, it was divided amongst the fang-bearing Dakinis into bowls made from the skulls of humanoids too large to be human and consumed by each of them. Now I experienced a phenomenon in which I existed within and as each of the Dakinis. At this realization of interconnectedness the entire vision imploded in a flash of light that arose out of complete darkness as a Tibetan syllable which glowed indigo and then I awoke.

I'll have plenty of time to reflect upon it as I walk but for now I must depart.

December 15th – Evening
I find myself continuously surprised at the great amount of trekkers present in the winter season. Even where I have departed from the common trails and roads it is not uncommon for me to spot a large tour group at least several times throughout the day. There have been a few villages throughout my journey thus far and a somewhat larger one yesterday that I avoided entirely so as to avoid any patrolmen. It seemed a haven for tourists in any case. I've been camping out in valley passes so as to avoid any detection and have thus far been entirely successful. At a point yesterday a man was calling out to me from a distance but I dared not risk my journey to respond to him and merely quickened my own pace for he could have been patrol, though I do hope he wasn't in need of any assistance. My food supply has not dwindled much and my energy is high, though I am feeling that a map would have

been a useful amenity to have purchased. I've weighed out the risks involved with stopping through a village to purchase a map and decided that it isn't worth the risk of being detained. Instead I have only the mountains and the sun, when it is visible, to guide me. It has been snowing but is yet to become a blizzard: for this I am thankful.

December 16th – Morning
I have yet another dream to transcribe from throughout the night. This one was perhaps more vague than the previous one that I wrote (I have since had other dreams but they appeared to belong to a more mundane sphere and were not worth transcribing). In a rather brief manner I was in a state of darkness or perhaps nothingness, the only disturbance being the deep chanting of monks in the Tibetan language. There was no particular sense of direction from which the chanting emerged but upon this observation there appeared all at once visual pulsations of vibrational waves, appearing in circular forms that expanded in breadth as they emerged from their invisible source. These appeared in the eight directions around me, as well as from above and below, and accordingly did they bring spatial definition to my state of nothingness. As the waves collided with me they reverberated back to their source, growing in expanse all the time and emanating outwards towards infinity, therefore defining infinite and limitless space in the process. Though I am not sure such emptiness could properly be called space but may be more accurately called a precursor to space. In any case, I have more exciting news.

Upon awakening and stepping outside of my tent to relieve myself I saw in the eastern distance a mountain, the top of which is a plateau upon which rested a great monastery. This may be the opportunity for what I am searching for! It interests me that I did not recognize it last evening but this was likely due to the white snow clouds that obscured my vision of the distant mountains. It is a fairly clear morning, much more so than it has been throughout the recent days and perhaps this is an optimistic sign of things to come.
I will proceed towards the mountain temple today and pending time will begin my ascent of it.

Evening
I've arrived at the foot of the mountain path only just now. So much for the clear morning; an hour or so later something of a blizzard passed through and made the hike a difficult one. It was difficult enough to walk the makeshift trail to the mountain and I had to rely on landmarks within close proximity, for the visibility was low. But I have made it to the bottom of the mountain and the blizzard has let up, leaving a gentle but steady snow in its wake. It took some time for me to circle the massive mountain until I found the narrow path that presumably leads to the top but here I am. Tomorrow morning I ascend up the mountain.

December 17th – Evening
No good! I ascended the mountain, or about 7/8th the way up at which point two of the monks, apparently Buddhists judging by their saffron and yellow robes, approached me. They were waiving their hands in a

gesture that I had foolishly interpreted initially as a greeting but once I had obtained visibility of their faces and the gesture itself I saw that they were essentially shooing me away. I attempted communication to explain myself but they would hear nothing of it and only spoke harshly in Tibetan before making threatening gestures, so I was forced to descend the circling path of the great mountain wholly unsatisfied. I admit to feeling discouragement right now. On my passage back down the mountain I wondered many times whether or not this entire journey was a mistake. I've considered whether my dreams were not prophetic after all and whether I acted rashly to come here and wander the Himalayas in search of spiritual initiation. Such are the thoughts of the discouraged, yet what keeps me going is the realization that I came here with the intention of initiation into Bon and not Buddhism, so perhaps this experience was meant to more firmly establish my alliance for the initiations that I seek. The sun was barely visible today, the sky and surrounding atmosphere being a perpetual white cloud, and as such I am not sure in truth what side of the mountain I am presently on. I will awake at dawn and follow the direction of the rising sun eastward as I continue my journey.

December 20th

I've found my way back east since I last wrote but the storms have only become worse. Thankfully the tempest of snow hasn't completely frozen some of the rivers yet and water has still been obtainable if I crack the surface sheet of ice, but I fear what will happen at this rate if I do not reach a hospitable destination soon. Alas, for the moment my canteen is full and keeping it on the inside of my coat has allowed the water to warm from its near freezing temperatures. My supply of dried meat is not yet running low though there has been a significant cleavage made in it. The warm and fragnant food at Kathmandu are but a distant memory as are the multitude of colors in their markets and architecture. Out here in this ice governed wasteland there naught but cold and immeasurable whiteness. Even the grey leafless winter trees do not dare to display their hue amidst the blanket of white for fear that a hidden purple hue may be discovered amidst them and in turn disturb the purity that the spirits of this place have crafted. I am the lone visitor in a home of wild spirits.

My thoughts throughout these eerie and secluded grey days have oft returned to the events that lead me to the present. Perhaps it is a mechanism of the mind to keep me going forward with optimism. It is just as well that I transpose some of them, for I had not at those times been in the habit of keeping a written journal and am at present stationary due to turbulent weather. My fascination with the spiritual sciences of the east began with my study of the Bardo Thodol; the Tibetan Book of the Dead. I performed the practices therein which ensure the vigilant practitioner to maintain wakening consciousness at the time of death so as to be aware and in control of the state in between death and rebirth into the next incarnation. It would also have it that the rituals brought about immense psychological transformation both due to the clearing of repressed mental blockages as well as the addition of considerable amounts of spiritual power endowed by the lineages of Buddhas, wrathful and peaceful beings, and Dakinis that the exercises connect one to.

I began to have fascinating dreams promptly upon my regular practice of the Bardo Thodol and many such dreams consisted of the wrathful deities appearing first in the forms of their artistic depiction before becoming terrible destructive storms that leveled cities of no particular familiarity to me. I considered with interpretation that these dreams represented the transformations occurring within my own psyche and that out of the ruin of the cities would emerge the newly integrated energies brought to me by Buddhism. I continued these practices and shortly thereafter was lead to discovering the system of Tibetan Bon. The practices that I learned from Bon were comparatively gentle when contrasted by those of Tibetan Buddhism of the Vajrayana path and indeed their inception was a more thorough sense of healing that I could comprehend more fully with my conscious mind. I experienced greater balance from Bon however the wrathful deities of Vajrayana Buddhism never departed from my energy field and have become something of a permanent integration (no wonder then that I have been caught in the midst of such infuriated storms!). Unfortunately, or perhaps fortunately, my literary resources for Bon were limited and very few have yet been translated into English. My options were to learn the Tibetan language and hope for the best in my discovery of Bon texts of practice or venture to Nepal where I had heard that the Bon continue to dwell. So it is that I am seeking initiation into a genuine lineage of Bon practitioners. In retrospect I hadn't really considered too extensively the obscurity of my approach to them as a Westerner speaking almost no Tibetan while requesting initiation into their mysteries but I do hope they show me compassion.

December 22th

I've stopped into a small rural village. I had to weigh the risks but decided it was necessary, considering that water has been scarce and my food supply is becoming lower than I feel comfortable with. Not a person here speaks a lick of English which is rare for villages throughout Nepal, but I was able to borrow a map from a young man by drawing one in the snow to indicate what I needed. He invited me into his home and prepared for me a warm cup of a delicious fruity tea made from herbs that were no doubt picked locally in the warmer months. As we looked over the map at the old wooden table in his humble home (the houses here tend to be small and simple; seemingly they are comprised of clay) I saw that our location was at the near north-eastern most point of Nepal. The labels upon the map were all written in Tibetan but I was able to point out Kathmandu and traced a rough outline of my path which has apparently been hugging the northern border of Nepal. It appears that this village, of which I know not the name, may have at one time been a part of the Kingdom of Tibet. It is a stroke of luck that I have avoided the patrolmen thus far being so north, though in the barren lands I have travelled through they would have no reason to be searching for tourists lacking the proper trekking permits. After a time when it felt that I was overstaying my welcome at the young man's home, I expressed a gesture of gratitude to him and departed to the market. There I purchased more preserved meats (which I was thankful that they offered for otherwise it would have been raw lentils) to last me several weeks. As I write I am sitting in a common area under a type of awning.

Evening
As I sat in the awning covered area earlier an intuition caused me to glance towards my left across a row of houses and I saw a man that held the appearance of a shaman or ngagpa. He wore his hair very long and demonstrated various bone and feather jewelry. The feathers undoubtedly were obtained in warmer times for I have not seen a bird since my arrival in Nepal. I approached him and to the best of my abilities made gestures upon the astral plane, hoping that he could perceive them with his second sight and hoping that they were not simply my imagination, to indicate that I was seeking initiation. He eyed me strangely for a moment and then seemed deep in thought as though pondering something. Then, with a sudden look of determination in his weather beaten eyes, followed by a brief laugh, he gestured for me to follow him. Needless to say I was joyed at the prospect and followed him to his home which was somewhat larger than the others and displayed an iron door with the markings of a silver sun and moon.

Inside his home was seated a lovely woman who I assumed to be his wife and who smiled at us as we entered though eyed me with a similar strange look that her husband had earlier. Around the house were various herbs and tools, few of which I could identify the use of. My smile must have given away my enthusiasm from a mile away. The ngagpa burned a great bowl of incense after gesturing for me to sit upon a straw mat and a few moments later the entire hut was dense with the smoke of various sage plants and jasmine flowers. He sat across from me and so thick was the smoke that I was scarcely able to make out the features of his face. I began to feel relaxed and was able to perceive a red glow at the level of his solar plexus, a blue glow at the level of his sacral chakra and a black glow at the root chakra beneath his feet. Beams of light from these chakras were projected towards my own chakras and I fell into a deep trance like state upon their connection. What happened next was incredibly vivid, the most so of any spirit journey I have ever taken out of body. The ngagpa and I were seated upon the great ocean of white clouds in the sky above and he spoke to me in his own language, which I now understood. He informed me that he could not initiate me himself but that the monastery where he once trained may accept me as a monk. I was told that I must travel to Bhutan to the Bon monastery and would find what I seek there. Without any time for me to interject we were suddenly riding upon the back of an enormous gold garuda bird across the skies. From this vantage point I was shown the trail that I was to follow so as to pass into Bhutan unnoticed and towards the location of the monastery.

The monastery itself was nested deep in the hollow of a valley, concealed by a massive cavern of stone from the remainder of the world. While atop the garuda in Bhutan the ngagpa informed me that this would be a kora or pilgrimage necessary for me to make in order to prove my worthiness for initiation, and I was ensured that the monks at the monastery would be able to recognize the path that I had taken to reach them. I was also informed that all of my earlier dreams alone did not guarantee me initiation but instead were often premonitions of potentiality.

The ngagpa has provided me with the mat to rest on tonight and I am anxious to continue my journey east to Bhutan tomorrow morning. It appears the journey was worth taking after all!

December 27th
I made it across the borders out of Nepal, through a tight pass in a strange region of India and into Bhutan. Will write again when I near the monastery.

December 30th
As I write I am standing at the edge of the valley that leads down into the cavern concealed monastery. It feels as though I am standing at the threshold of a place of great ancient power. The visions shown to me by the ngagpa have truly lead me here without a flaw, incredible.

January 1st
I've been accepted into the monastery without

obstruction. It was as though I was expected, for no one had come out to greet me along the steep valley leading down to it but several monks were awaiting me at the front gates. The architecture here is richly adorned with so many colors and the images of serpents are so intertwined into the intricate architecture. It is unlike any monastery I have ever seen pictures of. The monks of higher rank wear tall pointed grey hats. I do not speak their language but I've nicknamed them the Grey Hat Sect, in contrast to the colored hat sects of Buddhism. It is somehow appropriate considering the blizzards I have passed through recently as the dark grey color of their wool hats corresponds flawlessly with that of the sky above. I wonder if they practice extensive weather magick.

There is something strange about my stay here at present, namely that it seems as though I am being kept in a room secluded from the remainder of the monastery. I am in truth unsure of whether or not this is an aspect of the initiatory process or not. Any attempts to leave the room thus far are met by disagreeable monks and I hope that I have not made any offensive gesture in my attempts. The room I am in now is plain compared to the richly adorned monastery that is outside of it, bearing only a white wall up to my waste and dark grey above it. It reflects the snowy wastelands of nature here interestingly enough.

January 2nd
I experienced a most unusual and somewhat disturbing dream during the night. I was standing

outside in the central yard with many of the monks, who were chanting in a deep tone that bordered upon growling. A large round mandala formed of copper on the ground collapsed into a hollow that opened into a pit, seemingly by the power of their vocalized vibrations. A faint red glow came from the depths of the pit and suddenly an array of demons arose out from it. The demons, appearing like wrathful deities though harsher and resembling humans less so than is usual, encircled and wrapped me in chains adorned with Tibetan letters that I sensed to relay some violent message. I was adorned with blood stained blades of all shapes and at all areas of my body, and then this entire arrangement was cloaked in a grey light as though to conceal it. I awoke feeling fear from this experience for it was darker than any that I have thus far had and in truth my words have done it no justice.

Midday

I have just returned from a visionary session with one of the monks. I was escorted from my room into the dwelling area of several grey hats and in a similar manner to the ngagpa they burned thick incense after requesting that I consume the seeds of a thorny seedpod. In the vision three of the grey hats informed me that upon returning from the vision I was to leave the monastery at once and proceed north-east towards another temple that will be found nested in a mountain. I was shown an image of the mountain and was informed that the path would be straightforward once I had exited the valley. When I came out of the vision the grey hats had already departed and two of the younger monks escorted me back to my room. I am unsure as to why they insist that I depart right at this moment midday but if it is for my initiation then so be it, though I must admit that all of this is becoming confusing to me. My thoughts are occasionally tempted by the warmth of my own homeland but I will conquer the grip of samsara and make this land my own home. I depart now into a most viscous of storms to fulfill my destiny.

Night
The storm has cleared for the moment and for the first time since my arrival in Asia I see a vast open sky of stars. This would be stunningly beautiful were it not for a certain feeling that I cannot seem to shake concerning the ritual I experienced in my dream last night. That it was an actual ritual and not simply a dream, I have no doubt, and ever since its occurrence I have been afflicted by both a peculiar burning sensation in my lower chakras and a nausea that comes and goes.

January 4th
I arrived this afternoon at the monastery as I was directed. It was extremely concealed on the side of a mountain and had I not recognized the mountain from the previous visions I would have never noticed it. I was examined curiously by the monks as I made my way to the entrance but they sort of shrugged when looking at each other and let me in, appearing a little confused. Curiously this monastery is a Buddhist one rather than Bon and I am wondering how this is involved with the initiatory dynamics. I had no idea that they crossed

over so intricately but then I suppose there is plenty for me to learn seeing as so little has been translated for the west. I admit to feeling the extreme cultural boundaries ever since making contact with the ngagpa in the small Nepalese village.

The architecture and art here are different from that of the Bon monastery, being somewhat more peaceful in appearance and more richly adorned. In place of the images of violent wrathful demons dismembering humans and one another as was depicted at the Bon temple, here the art is comprised largely of peaceful bodhisattvas and a balance of wrathful and peaceful deities. It seems a place of greater balance in general and perhaps indicates that as part of my initiation I have entered a place of greater balance after climbing out of the pit in that cavernous hollow. Perhaps that was what the demons of the dream represented. In any case the architecture here is adorned with saffron and yellows and does not bear the serpentine curves of the Bon monastery but instead displays a more traditional or at least widely utilized stylization.

Interestingly enough I have been escorted into a room as I was at the previous monastery though there are no guards that prevent my coming and going as I please. The room itself is beautiful and luxurious: I have been welcomed with fine silks and pillows that allow for comfort I have scarcely experienced in a month's time or so. Silk tapestries of peaceful deities are adorned with jewels and fresh flowers, from where I have no idea, fill the room with a delightful fragrance.

I have analyzed the contrast between the plain room in which I was seemingly held captive against the present luxurious room where I am free to come and go. It appears to be a challenge of my notions of non-duality amidst variable circumstances of wantonness and simplicity. Perhaps my freedom to leave is a test of whether or not I would want to leave the luxuries of the world, and my desire to leave the plain room of imprisonment an exercise to harden my resolve in the face of obstacles so that I may ultimately see that in either circumstance all is but the emanations of samsara.

In general when I have departed my room the monks have for the most part avoided any eye contact with me. A few of the higher ranked monks, distinguished by black hats, eye me sternly but have not voiced a word to me nor invited me to commune with them privately. In fact if I knew no better I would have interpreted their glares as a look of malice. Surely this is all a test of my reserve though. The thought came to me today that perhaps I fulfill a prophecy predicted by lamas some time ago, as have many future lamas and Buddhas been predicted long before their arrival. Perhaps I am to represent a new type of Buddha who hails from the west and transcends the initiatory structure in its linguistically limited boundaries. This remains to be seen.

January 5th
A terrible dream. I walked out into the common areas of the monastery and from without me was projected

the chains of Tibetan letters that the demons had adorned me with some nights prior. They appeared as many headed naga serpents whose heads sprouted in multiplicity of form and color and throughout their slithering around the monastery inflicted harm and illness upon all of the monks. Many of the monks attempted to battle the nagas but without avail. I have yet to depart my room today and fear persecution should my dream have been true.

A short while later
It's a disaster! The monastery has fallen under a spell of sickness that none here appear to be exempt from. Many of the monks lay on the ground and I was unable to help any of them to stand. They all carry a strange green hue upon their skin and I fear that I have taken in me a touch of their sickness. I've returned to my room to rest and will write when there is some resolve to this.

The nausea that I have been feeling has turned to vomiting and it appears by my hands that my skin has taken on the familiar green hue. I am very weak and fear that I may not recover. So much confusion but I do not regret the journey. Om Mahakala Hum Phat!

Afterword:
This journal was initially discovered amongst the wares of a Nepalese market at Patan. It arrived there with a collection of relics obtained from an abandoned monastery that had apparently suffered an epidemic some twenty five years prior. Due to the isolation of

the monastery the discovery of the deceased did not occur for many years after the epidemic at which time whatever relics remained were distributed amongst local merchants and by some curious circumstances involving a gambling debt owed by one merchant to another the collection arrived nearly intact to Nepal from Bhutan. The story that accompanied the wares is that the monastery from which they were extracted was discovered to be ridden with corpses who had been mutilated, often missing limbs and other appendages. Another object of fascination was a tattoo upon the scalped skulls of each of the corpses that resembled the sun-like symbol often carved upon the sahasrara chakra of the deceased though in this instance displayed a type of black decay unanimously amongst the inhabitants of the monastery. It was initially thought that a group of savages had raided the monastery and murdered the monks, whose bodies had by then been decaying for several years.

Amidst the relics surrounding it the red leather-bound journal appeared conspicuous and caught the interest of a Tibetan scholar who spoke and read fluent English. He purchased the journal due to his curiosity and was able to trace several of its locations to monasteries and villages in Nepal and Bhutan, yet the mysterious "Grey Hat Sect" as the nameless narrator of the journal called them has never been discovered. The following is an account of what was speculated to comprise the experiences of the journal's narrator from the point of view of the scholar:

When he arrived at the small village, which will remain unnamed along with the remainder of the locations so as not to disturb their isolated inhabitants, it appears that the ngagpa took advantage of the young tourist's enthusiasm and sent him as a willing vessel to the thus-far unknown cavern bound monastery with whom the ngagpa was associated. When he arrived there he was detained in something of a prison quarters and eventually a ritual was performed so as to bind him as a walking and living curse. The chains that the demons of the pit utilized represented a binding of the narrator to matter while the Tibetan scripts that adorned them would have described the desired effects of the curse. The sharp weapons and tools placed upon him have been used by many sects for either protection or offense. As soon as he was shown his destination by the monks of the Grey Hat Sect he was sent on his way so that they would avoid the effects of the curse for themselves, and by all intents it appears that he was sent to a rival monastery.

Upon arriving at the rival monastery the charms which were placed upon him must have somehow disarmed the perceptions of the resident monks there who appeared to have taken him in under the guise of confusion concerning his reason for visitation. This undoubtedly was a premeditated component of the curse scripts; it is unfortunate that no written copy of the curse was transcribed though there are similar examples throughout the Himalayas and often an amulet designed to heal a curse or illness can simply be reversed to cause affliction. The Buddhist monks did not seem to fully suspect that the narrator had been cursed by the Bon clan in the cavern and as such the premeditated attack caught them entirely off guard and in turn brought death upon the entire monastery and the narrator of the journal as well.

Sorcerous battles have been commonplace between rival sects of Buddhism and Bon for thousands of years and continue to endure into the present as was demonstrated by their description in this journal, apparently unbeknownst to the scribe who believed he was taking part in an initiatory experience designed by the Bon Po. The tourist in this instance was simply a willing pawn in what was likely an ancient battle between rival sects, though no further evidence of any such "Grey Hat Sect" exists and presumably the sorcery that they practice has maintained their location in a state of concealment so that even today where the Himalayas have been charted thoroughly their presence remains a mere speculation.

Despite the untimely death of the narrator and all who comprised the Buddhist monastery it does appear that the narrator's speculations of taking part in a type of initiation were not entirely false. Death based initiations have been a part of various Vamamarga, Kapalika and later Vajrayana sects in South East Asia for millennia. In this instance it appeared that the rivalry between the sects was so strong that the Grey Hat Sect appeared to have visited the Buddhist monastery shortly after they obtained knowledge of the success of the curse, likely obtained from a visionary experience. Evidence suggests that they performed rites to block the sahasrara chakra of each of the monks and the narrator of the journal while harvesting bones from each of them, the likely function being the enslavement of the monks and narrator as spirit servants who would be without the ability to ascend beyond the denser emanations of samsara. This too is as uncommon of a practice as some may suppose and the Buddhas themselves were known to recruit various types of spirit servants. This practice eventually took on qualities that some would say were corrupted and in particular carried over from certain ancient sects of Bon, often finding their influence into later sects of Vajrayana Buddhism. The initiation that the narrator may have likely and unknowingly accepted then was his transformation into a spirit servant. His bones like those of the other monks were likely to be utilized as talismans to summon their spirits which would have undergone transformation into a denser and hence more demonic state of being as a result of the curse.

A relic left behind by a 17th century priest of the Drepung monastery in Tibet is that of a large dark grey pointed hat, similar in fashion to what was described by the narrator of the journal concerning the supposed Grey Hat Sect. This priest, called

Sonam Drakpa, eventually became the controversial deity Dorje Shugden after taking his own life and becoming a vengeful spirit. H.H. the 14th Dalai Lama has explicitly forbade any practice of Dorje Shugden and it must be speculated as to whether or not he in fact held relation to the Grey Hat Sect and may have penetrated the ranks of the Gelug monastery during the time of the fifth Dalai Lama as an act of war on their behalf. It was said that at the time of his death he predicted a tremendous black cloud to form in the sky above the pillar in which he was cremated and accounts for the occurrence of such a cloud exist. Diseases were then spread across numerous villages and monasteries and were historically attributed to Sonam Drakpa in the demonic form he had taken. If there is indeed any relation between Dorje Shugden and the Grey Hat Sect it may perhaps open the doors to an expanded study of malevolence and espionage amongst sects of Bon and Buddhism, the hostility of which has continued to this day.

The Trial of Frater Mark

The following diary was discovered amongst the belongings of Mark Schoorel and appears to have been intended as a diary maintained for the purpose of instruction to seekers of the so called occult sciences. It appears however that prior to his disappearance he diverged from his intended course of teaching and into a state of obsession beyond that which he clearly already suffered from. Despite the obvious suffering this man was undergoing throughout its writing, the brief diary is being released to the public due to requests received by the fellow practitioners of the so called occult sciences who were Mark Schoorel's acquaintances and more importantly with the hope that it may lead to information pertaining to his whereabouts.

5/20/2014 - Foreword to the Working
I have never been one to contemplate morality in my actions. When I joined my magickal order and swiftly

ascended the ranks it was, in my opinion, due to that very quality which many, at their own loss, may consider with such feeble concepts as sociopathic tendencies and sadism. I have watched so many others spend unnecessary years fumbling through their own self-doubts and social standards of moral that they scarcely learn or even experience a thing, and yet I armed only with a vigilant curiosity, ambition and no sense of guilt have courageously confronted the darkest tunnels of my own personal hell and arose from its center in the purest light as did Dante before me. The question does often arise to the student of the occult concerning what exactly it is that one does once they have accomplished the Great Work of the O.:.A and it is in this diary that I will attempt to record several processes concerning the work of a master adept, myself being distinguished amongst the great Adepts of our time.

5/24/2014

7:00 PM – I have been fasting from any food for three days and have been perfumed all throughout with the musky scents of the working which is in the nature of Saturn with Saturn in its retrograde phase, effectively allowing for the boundaries between the worlds to be at their thinnest, a desirable dynamic for the present working. My time has been spent in solitude and my retirement from the world has been sponsored by a fellow member of the Order. The work itself will exhibit the binding and extracting of knowledge from the Goetic Demon Aamon, itself a demon of the lunar alignment and bound under the angel Achasiah whose seal has been worn on my body throughout the previous three days. The working will begin tonight in the shadow hours.

10:00 PM through 2:00 AM – The working was something of a success and proceeded as follows:
I entered the temple dressed in the black silk robe and armed with the magickal weapons. The temple was dressed according to the necessary amenities of black and violet draperies and candles, as well as great quantities of musk and jasmine incense. I performed the LBRP and LBRH within the central circle of the temple and proceeded to recite the Conjuration while bearing the silver seal of the demon. As I spoke the words that resonated throughout the increasingly thick smoke of the room which overcame my senses at the most base instinctive faculties there began to appear in the triangle of arte the form of a wolf. The relative ease at which the demon appeared is noted. Armed with the sword I command the demon to reveal its true nature, and at once does a serpent appear as extending from the tail of the wolf, as flames subtly expel from the mouth of the beast.

I inquire as to whether this is the true form of the demon and it replies a simple "yes", and knowing this to be untrue I cast the iron bounding chains upon it and as it howls in pain I bellow the harsher secondary conjurations until the demon reveals its form as that of a raven gnashing carnivorous teeth. The raven appears in the triangle of arte as solidly as any object in the temple. It is worth noting the cold sensation that accompanied this phenomenon, no doubt the effect of the experience upon my own blood chemistry wherein the demon must draw upon whatever life force is around it in order to maintain its tangible form.

I loosen not the chains that bind this beast but only inquire about that which I have conjured it for; namely information regarding my own future, for such knowledge is of great value to me during a time such as this wherein the effects of time itself appear to be loosened. My inquiry was met by the beast offering to demonstrate my answer with visions, to which I complied. Projected around the bounds of the triangle of arte was the following scene:

I am standing in the temple not unlike as it presently is, though the working is apparently one of Saturn for all is blackened. My appearance is somewhat pale and gaunt and I seem to be in a sort of obsessed state. I am calling out a conjuration to the spirit and a type of black shapeless bulk appears in the triangle of arte. I attempt to bind it with chains and sword but to no avail and it quickly overcomes the boundaries of the triangle and myself.

At this point I banish the vision and beat the demon with the iron chains, commanding him in the proper tones to reveal truth rather than illusion. The demon insists that what he has shown me is genuine and I proceed to recite the third and harshest conjuration upon the lying beast whose screams have only become more horrible at this time. The demon agrees to show me the future more genuinely and once again projects the vision, though now it transcends the boundaries of the triangle outwards into the entire room. This was not what I requested but I did not interfere with the process, myself admittedly fascinated by the lucidity of this phenomenon and now a bit drowsy as though being lulled into hypnogogia. The second vision was as follows:

The environment is hell-like, akin to the forbidden realms of Quuth as I have explored previously, though this particular region I do not recognize despite its vague familiarity. It appears as a vast and ancient tunneled sewer system with several rivers flowing, though upon closer inspection the rivers flow not with water but instead with a type of darkened blood-like fluid flowing and coagulating along the river bank. This is reminiscent to me of blood arteries becoming corrupted by an influx flow of dark impurities. There are sadistic noises as though someone is being tortured, though I cannot see them and within my field of vision see only a black bulk of what appears to be randomly assorted organic matter pulsating on the ground. At the sight of this thing I feel a tinge of fear and with the fear the vision becomes increasingly lucid so that I no longer perceive any indication of the temple. I begin to walk, not daring to question my own form at present for fear that I may become as that shapeless mass.

The tunnel walls are rounded and covered with a type of unidentifiable sludge that was not quite static in nature. Colors in this place are difficult to distinguish and aside from an occasional darkened violet accent subtly impressed upon the river there is only blackness. A mist appears and overcomes all other vision and when it clears I am standing in a desert of black sand, gazing out into a clear night sky looming only with dark stars emitting their black light upon this cosmos. A dim violet moon in its full phase hangs in the sky, casting its aura upon the sands. There is an air of loneliness and isolation. Something in the corner of my eye prompts me to turn to the right and I perceive a grand obsidian pyramid in the distance. I venture towards this and am carried more quickly than expected along a black mist. Standing at the edge of the pyramid, I find no entrance. In vain I search its massive perimeter but find no visible entrance. The obsidian glass reflects the subtle violet aura of the moon upon my own face and the vision begins to fade so that I am standing back in the temple room amidst thick smoke, weighed down by a heavy sense of longing for the unattainable.

The demon asks to be given its license for departure but I am not in a good mood and refuse it's request, instead choosing to bind it permanently to one of the brass vessels prepared for demons to be enslaved. I force the pathetic beast into the vessel by the sword and despite its screams and furious gnashing it complies with sadness and I place the vessel upon a plate of iron aside the legion of others whom I have enslaved. The howling of these demons never ceases but even such pitiful beings have their uses to the adept. Feeling tired and exhausted, I venture to sleep without banishing rituals of any form.

6/4/2014

5:00 PM – I came down with an unexpected bout of illness following the prior working and have not written or done much else, truth be told. Such is the price of the Great Work when the darker arts are consulted. I must look a gout mess but no matter as the work must continue. The working tonight will be of the Mercurial alignment and I have already taken the steps to augment the temple for the working, decorating it with orange tapestries and eight pointed apparatus. The eight Goetia vessels are already placed upon their iron plates around the central circle. The direction of this recorded working, initially intended as a means to demonstrate the physical materialization of spirits, has undergone a change in that the Goetia are to be utilized as a sacrificial offering during the working tonight. During my recent days of bed-rest I was met with many dreams and visions of beings called the Archons. They did not interact with me directly but instead I was informed of their existence by a group of nameless extraterrestrial beings. My own ambitious curiosity is calling for me to pursue them and as such will I make an appropriate offering for their visitation tonight.

The extraterrestrial cult which I have been in communication with through dreams has informed me of specific ritual instructions through which I may establish a direct waking communication with them and thence to the Archons. The rite involves the use of the magick mirror and apart from the sacrificial offering of the eight Goetia there is to be a personal blood offering upon the obsidian mirror prior to its placement into the triangle of arte wherein the extraterrestrial cult has informed me will emerge a member from amongst their ranks. They instructed me too in regard to the necessary perfumes and incense; a curious tincture of baneful herbs not unlike certain flying ointments of old. A sigil was impressed upon me throughout all of our meetings so that I may remember and reproduce it and during the rite it is to be carved upon my abdomen to allow for the release of the blood offering.

This image is also to be painted on a large banner and placed at the north direction of the temple area. The eight enslaved Goetia are to be released after opening the triangle of arte to the extraterrestrial intelligence and offered as a gift to what is summoned so that it may be conveyed to the Archons. From there it is promised that I will be taken to a place upon Quuth where the Archons reside. The rite will commence at midnight tonight.

Here ends the diary entries. It is presumed that upon performing the "ritual", Mr. Schoorel in a state of delusion brought about by delirium inducing plant drugs likely departed the premises of his home, believing himself to have taken part in an extraterrestrial abduction in his state of mania. Any information regarding his whereabouts or anyone with whom he was in contact during the period of the dates transcribed within this diary should contact a local Richmond County police department.

The Hyperborean Isle of Rashuth

"What did you think of it?" Harold asked David as they walked to David's car in the movie theater parking lot. The two friends had just spent three hours watching the new Pembu-Carbonica movie, part of a franchise about large shape-shifting life forms comprised of lead and their interactions with humanity. "It was okay, probably a little long though. I would have been content if they cut it down about an hour" replied David. They found their vehicle amongst the countless insect-like metallic rectangles, or modern automobiles that comprised the streetlight lit parking lot that evening and rushed to escape the coming traffic of exiting the lot. In a somewhat desperate maneuver they speeded out through the rear exit of the lot which faced a forest that few ventured into, and departed onto the highway in the opposite direction to their home. At this point in time the exponentially inflating human volume upon Richmond County had made it so that it was something of an ordeal to travel any distance across the relatively small island, itself only approximately fifteen miles in length. Only twenty years earlier this island had been nearly barren with human life and flourishing with plant and animal life, yet in recent times and with an unforeseen mass migration of citizens from nearby regions this had changed and a balance between the natural world and the human artifice was constructed.

As the two young men drove towards the western region of the island, much of it being comprised of uninhabitable swamp lands that rung a tone reminiscent of primordial pasts, they soon found themselves lost: in itself an unusual event upon such a small island. Perhaps it was due to the fact that Harold had produced marijuana soon after they departed the movie theater parking lot, apparently a new product that he had purchased earlier that day he told David who himself was not much of a recreational drug user. Nevertheless, they both smoked and soon found themselves in an area of Richmond County that they were entirely unfamiliar with.

As they slowed down their car on the small one lane road they observed a house to their left that appeared without lights and had an air of the colonial homes that had existed here several hundred years prior. They observed the house for a moment before hearing what sounded like a strange high-pitched croak, at which point they sped around the tight bend of a road and found a moment later that they had merged onto an unpaved road in a thick forest, nearly as dense as a jungle. David inquired, "Where are we?" to which Harold responded, "In a place not often troubled by humankind I suspect". Their conversation which may have otherwise taken a philosophical direction was cut short by the sound of the wheels spinning without movement, and they realized after a brief paranoid moment that they were caught in the mud. David shook his head, "Of all place to be stuck in the mud, I'm not even sure how a tow truck would make it into here". Harold exited the car and attempted to push the car while David held the gas, but this was futile and resulted only in Harold having been covered in thick black mud.

At this time David exited the car and they agreed upon walking to find help, as their cellular phones received no signal. They walked the way they had come yet it was a few short moments later that the road itself seemed to have disappeared and the jungle grew thicker. They tried in vain to retrace their steps back to the car but without avail and, standing in the middle of a misplaced jungle whose natural sounds of unusual insects and unidentifiable reptiles and mammals became an exceedingly dominant vibration. Quickly losing their sense of coordination amongst the strange night environment and due to tiredness and intoxication they decided to simply choose a direction and walk, believing that they would eventually discover an indication of modern human civilization. This too proved far more difficult than such a simple task would appear, for it was as though the trees themselves twisted and turned with an abnormal rapidity for such beings that exhibited normally moderate movement. With the jungle itself seeming to create an unsolvable labyrinth for them, the two young men walked for some time and in no particular direction.

It was around the time of dawn, both suffering from severe exhaustion and thirst by now, that they began to notice the first changes in their skin: it was becoming somewhat hardened and sleek, resembling vaguely the scales of certain monitor lizards. This realization left them bewildered yet in their sleep deprived and still intoxicated state they accepted the changes reasonably well, determined to discover a touch of humanity in a place devoid of it. As the sun gradually climbed above the horizon the appearance of their environment however took a far greater toll upon their mental states, for around them was thick and towering plant life unlike any that could have rationally grown in their region, and during several occasions was there cast a great winged shadow from somewhere high above, accompanied by a sort of rhythmic beating vibration akin to that of wings, though the wings of what they dared only to speculate.

Many creatures unheard during the night began to stir as a reddish golden hue was established firmly upon the sky above them, seen only through the thick ceiling of trees. Twice they caught sight of serpents much too large to exist according to any rational thought, at which they quickly chose an alternative direction to move; by this time they had forsaken all hope of walking in a particular direction and their venture had become something of a frenzied passage. A sound of chanting caught their ears and they agreed that it may be best to avoid its direction, yet it appeared that despite their attempts at avoidance the jungle would repeatedly direct them to an area within earshot of the unusual chanting. It was Harold who made out some of what was being said, which was chanted in an unknown language:

U'l Aba'a Khaphrash Shutah! Shifoth Turqa'a Minash Shafah! Undaqa Fatas Shimok Lalung!

And this bizarre chant continued in its offbeat fashion, heightening in volume no matter the path that the two young men chose until within their field of vision they perceived a remarkable sight: a village comprised of some ancient and unknown construction, whose buildings appeared shaped to resemble conic-volcanoes and each similarly maintaining an opening at its roof. The inhabitants of the village were however of a far more astounding sight, for they appeared to represent humanoids in a far earlier or perhaps entirely distant stage and stream of development. These beings appeared scaled as reptiles yet displayed hair and somewhat hominid type features that predated any bone structure known to modern human biologists. They were entirely nude save for the bones and sinew worn upon their bodies for some necromantic purpose. Harold, himself a student of biology, was immensely fascinated despite the nature of their circumstances for such a genetic diversity manifest in the phenotype was scarcely observed in such an unrestrained form. He noted to himself then that the scales that had appeared upon David and himself were likely the result of an Archaea strain of bacteria in this strange environment which, having become infused with their own microbial genomes, would have produced an unusually high rate of mutation apparently necessary for survival in this environment. The nature of the environment itself he scarcely was concerned with now, for the diversity of life there had begun to occupy his observations now that the red sky above them clearly illuminated the area.

David on the other hand was far less enthusiastic about their situation and saw all too well the severity that they were potentially involved with. He quietly said to Harold "We have to avoid those beings; they are most likely dangerous living rurally in a place like this" to which Harold agreed was true in all probability but upon turning to depart found that a myriad of large reptiles and serpents of an almost extraterrestrial design were shifting around them and a few appeared to advance towards them. Given the option of facing carnal creatures of the jungle or the tribe who were potentially of a more civilized design, they promptly chose to enter the village and sprinted across the small distance to it, overstepping a large serpent along the way.

As they cautiously entered the village the chanting did not cease, save for a few amongst them who eyed them with strange excitement, and the two watched as their morning ceremony in which an archaic cauldron filled with blood and herbs was boiled and dumped at the borders of the village at four directions. Concluding the ceremony the two young men, having been somewhat lulled into a false sense of security, were seized and carried into one of the volcanic shaped huts. Several moments later three females of the tribe entered the hut and eyed the two young men with a look that could have either been lust or hunger, perhaps both, and proceeded to remove Harold from the hut and relocate him elsewhere.

David was now facing a male who, judging by the vast array of bones he was adorned with was a type of shamanic hunter. The eerily yellow eyes set into the scaled and hairy face of this being eyed David as though seizing him up in all ways and then, having spoken a few strange words to the male restraining David, walked to the corner of the hut from which he produced a long bone that terminated with an immense and wicked razor-like claw. David was entirely frightened at what would come next and after handing this weapon to the male that restrained David they walked to the outskirts of the village, being eyed all the way by the villagers. Once upon the outskirts the male let David loose and, producing the weapon, handed it to him and motioned for him to depart. David thanked him futilely in the English tongue, believing he was being set free, and ran off into the jungle with the clawed weapon.

Harold meanwhile had been reduced to nakedness and was taking part in a forced breeding with the three females. This was of the most unusual sexual intercourse that he had ever experienced for, aside from the bestial nature of the females, their genitalia resembled that of many reptiles in that it was concealed within an open slit upon their underside. Amidst alien scents and sounds he was forced beyond the brink of exhaustion, a point he had reached hours long before, to reproduce with these females as though to ensure their pregnancy. This occurred while a group of males observed with jealous eyes and Harold feared what may come due to jealous outrage yet all the while could not help but find fascination in the idea of spreading his own genetic line under such extraordinary circumstances. This pattern was continuously forced upon him for three days, allowing him periods of rest during the night where he was well guarded by irritated males of the village who did not restrain themselves from occasionally striking him with their bone clubs.

David had not found any solace during this time and during any attempt at rest was met only with an expanse of strange insect bites upon awakening or was otherwise awoken from his half-sleep by some strange sound or heavy vibrations upon the earth, as though created by the footsteps of some colossal and unrestrained beings. On the third day he was awoken by such footsteps and perceived with horror their source: the shaman hunter of the village, accompanied by the other two males he had earlier been restrained by with Harold, advanced through the jungle upon the back of a large beast that appeared in mass like an elephant yet bared the striped flesh of certain felines which was comprised of scales that reflected the red light of the sky above it and the green light of the plants that it trampled below it.

Believing at first that it had been found out that the male set him free, a darker thought came over him: he was intentionally let free so that he could be hunted. He quickly set himself down from the tree he had been resting in, thankful for the dexterity he had developed as a child, and sprinted towards an arrangement of boulders he had seen in the distance with the hope that he may hide amongst them. This was met with success for a crevice was discovered underneath one of the great bluish stones and crawling through it he found himself in a hollow cavernous arrangement amidst the boulders. The area was uninhabited save for a spider the size of his torso that he never let his eyes off of and which eyed him with an apparent malice. He listened as the booming footsteps of that great beast neared and then departed, leaving the sounds of great insects and reptiles in their wake.

Harold on his third day of successive mating had become exhausted to the degree of near-insanity and in a fit of desperation drew the clawed club of a nearby male during a time when very few were in the hut and, after slaying one of the women and two men, spurted from the village and into the jungle without looking back. He was unsure of where this burst of energy had arisen from but it was as though a stream of primal predatory instincts had finally overwhelmed the mental wanderings of reason that occupied him previously. He was ignorant to the circumstances of his friend David, assuming he had either been placed into a similar situation as him or had been sacrificed for the blood offering observed days earlier, and set off into the jungle only with the purpose of creating distance between himself and anything appearing civilized in this place, for he now felt more secure amidst the untamed creatures of nature. This attitude began to fade during the forthcoming days where bulky insects often flew into him to tear at his flesh and he began to wonder if perhaps he had prematurely sacrificed his shelter in the village.

Chance would have it that Harold, seeking a stable shelter in which he could rest, happened upon the boulder arrangement and found David inside of it. The spider that had once been there had been slaughtered for food and what little of it remained they both feasted on before retiring into a genuine slumber, without so much of a word spoken concerning the preceding events. They awoke after a period of time they could not estimate and saw that the sky now had taken on a greenish hue and for the first time saw the moon hanging full in the sky, yet whirling rapidly upon its wobbling axis and traversing the sky in its entirety in only twenty minute intervals or so. It was decided that they would have no choice but to venture from this place of solitude which for them had acquired a sort of sacred eminence due to the protection they found there.

During the fortnight, they hunted and consumed several of the smaller sized reptiles, always avoiding the larger amongst them, and gradually the more basic instincts of their genes became dominant, possessed with the primal ways long since forgotten by most. It was after this period of time that they reached the sea. Weighing the risks involved, they agreed to build a small fire so that they could cook the large ammonite-like shellfish that combed the beach there. Harold noted that these types of life forms existed at least 66 million years in the past according to their evolutionary timeline and the very real nature of what had occurred for them began to set in, though they did not in the least understand the dynamics of its occurrence.

They remained at the sea for some time undisturbed and were able to obtain much needed rest and regeneration. For water, they had found a nearby stream that ran from the jungle into the ocean and without any choice drank from it. Occasionally a huge stirring in the ocean would occur and from under its surface would rise the head of some unidentifiable creature of the ancient seas, but these creatures maintained a fair distance from the shore, terrifying as they may be. Several lunar phases later, at a time increment they were thus far without luck in calculating, an enormous mass of gelatinous and transparent blue appeared at the surface of the ocean at a near distance. It remained this way for the course of several following days with the only anomaly being a countless quantity of smaller beings of its type appearing upon the coast and proceeding into the jungle without any displayed interest into the two young humans there. Their strange luminescence was fascinating but was not seen since in the coming days and only appeared, all throughout the day and night, upon the gargantuan being that appeared to be a type of jellyfish. A fortnight from this time, the great gelatinous mass spoke to Harold and

David telepathically and its voice was heard after what could be described as a suction seemed to draw in a strange electrical fluid that, once circulated through the brain and blood, allowed the voice of the great jellyfish to be heard with clarity in their own minds. It spoke in a warbled voice that held the acoustics of electrified metal such as that of a spark gap:

"I am Dorin, one of nine high emperors of the Dorinias Kingdom. Our people keep and maintain the memories of time at the ocean's bottom, concerning all that has come and all that is yet to come. Time is of course in a state of constant fluctuation much like all of nature and as such our responsibility is considerably pervasive. I do trust that my dialect is understood clearly, for there is knowledge that we wish to impart upon you"

"Long predating the development of your modern multicellular life forms, during a shadow of time when the moon rounded the earth at exceedingly rapid and unpredictable velocities and strange form bearing mists hung freely upon the earth's surface; where primordial stews were disturbed by the perturbations of extraterrestrial phenotypes, the natural emergences of this earth were to be found in their untempered and boundless manifestations".

"The initial biological organizations of the earth, in an inevitable bout of irony, first appeared by means of an otherworldy asteroid upon which ectoplasmic fog became congealed in geometric ice; a primitive exemplar of what human alchemists have called the great work, accomplished by prokaryotes. The collision of this primeval cellular life with the primordial earthly wastelands stimulated an unrestricted renaissance of living development. The nature of earth, for nature is a relative term not bound to any singular system, soon thereafter proceeded to the formulation of its early multicellular life forms, the single cells having devoured their bacterial associates to allow for unlimited potentiality of power to be biologically generated by symbiotic mutation".

"Earthly nature created as its offspring a parthenogenetic zygote of predatory creatures that drank from the azoth of the fallen flame and preserved it in an undisturbed manner. There were however other disturbances to occur and these would be initiated by intelligences of a differing nature, belonging to alternative lines of evolution and substance. When the Hireinic Protogenus, as they wished to become known, arrived upon the earth, they were dissatisfied with the genetic developments then established and began their own experimentations. While the creatures of nature were excessively large and predatory, the Protogenus crafted forms that could be more easily contained and as such the hermaphrodite azoth of earthly nature became split asunder, creating myriad emanations under comparatively limited and controlled circumstance. It would be a very long time before the unbounded expressions of the primordial stew would become manifest once again, for the concentration of their reign was limited by an earthly division of interests. There were the primeval predatory species that desired to rule in this world and ascend towards those above it at expedient rates, contrasted by those more accommodating to the Protogenus influence that desired evolution of a more lofty and gradual sequencing".

"In time the Melkrasha, kin to ancient Protogenus, initiated a conquest to the reemergence of the unrestrained expressions of the azoth. These ineffably ancient and powerful beings invoked a predatory nature within themselves, feeding upon the creations of the Protogenus; an act that ruptured their relationship with Hireinic law and initiated the plummet of an evolutionary age. The predatory nature of the unrestrained was without evolutionary means, for it did not require alteration or improvement, yet the Melkrasha discovered and tempered methods to evolution out of the dark wastes of Qu'uth by utilizing the Penumbra of the Archons. The Melkrasha were themselves a bureau of the Archons that arose within the world of Malk. In time the Melkrasha brought unbalance to the evolutionary progress of the world and in turn your homo- sapiens species was stricken heavily by their influence; yet amongst your species are distributed many ancient remnants of the Hireins, including their bureau the Protogenus. This fact in itself alludes to great war and conflict amongst your people, for there exists within your very genomes a conflict of priorities that began long ago as a cosmic strife and in your quarantined time sphere continues to enact through your species".

This dialogue reawakened the human thought faculties

in Harold and enchanted his mind by the curious awe of the world. He thought to himself that this strange being Dorin spoke very eloquent English for a being who had likely never communed with a human, though he was unaware that the languages spoken through telepathy would be automatically transliterated to accommodate the ears of the listener. David, more concerned with his state of impoverishment and experiencing a touch of madness from all that he was hearing, asked the question "Why are you speaking to us of these matters"? Dorin continued:

"The renaissance of life in your own time has all but ceased due to its strict limitations. Having precognitively foreseen this event it is essential that the ancient seeded memories within your genomes become reawakened now, so that when you depart from Rashuth and return to your own time and place this knowledge may be electromagnetically broadcasted from your own phenotypes onto others of your species and the world around you in order to remind it of its antiquity."

Frustrated, David asked "How exactly should we intend on returning to our place and time"? Dorin responded firmly and impatiently, "It will be done soon" and at that submerged itself and sent a large wave to crash onto the beach. The wave carried the two young men back into the jungle, they having lost their grounding, and as if by a miracle found themselves back at the car they had entered this place with. It was night and the sky was dark blue, illuminated in the nearby distance by the yellow ambiance of street lights. The immense wall of sound found in the jungle was reduced to the chirping of crickets and they saw that the road behind them was as clear as ever. According to a yellow sign, they had arrived at an island park dedicated to preserving swamplands and forest and they saw that the road behind them was as clear and paved.

Harold said genuinely "Well that was interesting" as they entered the car and drove home, having sobered from the marijuana and unsure of just how what seemed like a month or more in a strange land had passed in a matter of hours. Harold noticed a text message on his phone and saw that his drug dealer had sold him the wrong bag of marijuana accidently and warned him not to smoke it because it contained an experimental hallucinogenic drug DOT-18. Harold never did inform David of this however for despite the fact that the experience had been hallucinatory he felt that there was genuine relevance to the experience and that they had each accessed some ancient part of themselves and their environment. The phenomenon of telepathy had occurred to several degrees for they had shared similar visions throughout much of the experience and later recounted an almost identical message spoken to them by an enormous jellyfish. Needless to say, nearly anyone that they attempted to convey this message to thought them to be mad, though a few received it with an open heart and mind; perhaps those who needed to hear it most in order to reawaken the ancient purposes presented to their genome long ago.

Meanderings of a Wicked Soul

The Green Harlequin

Part 1

I very rarely become sick and even pride myself somewhat upon having an uncommonly strong immune system. Invariably, this is simply due to the diversity of my genome, as well as preventative measures that I take daily in the form of a healthy diet. I also refrain, and have for many years, from the consumption of any antibiotics, so as to secure myself with a strong immune system. Nonetheless, and in the midst of an unusually bad flu season, I experienced for the first time in my life the phenomenon of influenza.

On the odd occasion that I do fall ill I tend to perceive it as a purging process; it is true that such ailments do tend to coincide with significant changes in my life, most often being those of a psychological nature.

This occasion was no different. At the time I had been on the verge of entering into my Master's studies in philosophy. It was my intention to become a professor and to otherwise have some greater credentials behind my written works. Truth be told, I despised the necessity of credentials which civilization had imposed, but then I likewise despised, and altogether feared, civilization in general.

You see, I am of an immensely introverted nature. The Myers-Briggs personality assessment labels me as an INFJ, that is, introverted-intuitive-feeling-judging. My personality represents perhaps 1% of the total human population, although that number may be generous. This world is not designed for people like me. It is, rather, designed by and for the extroverted types, those with great ambitions to achieve greatness in the context of values which are not their own. It is only the introverted types who endeavor to establish our own standard of values, and none are more prone to this than those belonging to my own personality type.

I was never really ambitious about very much in this world. It isn't that I didn't take joy from certain things; I am something of an accomplished musician, artist and writer. Nonetheless it was always very difficult for me to have my abilities recognized by the world. After all, I maintain the utmost creative integrity to myself alone and am entirely uncompromising on this point. I do not expect that very many people understood my writings, artworks or musical compositions, but for me they have always represented the forefront of genuine creative expression.

Without much ambition it was very difficult for me to secure work for myself. I was generally unwilling to lower myself to the barbarian cutthroat manner of behavior maintained by most humans in the workplace. Neither did I get along very well with coworkers in most instances. There were always one or two with whom I could experience friendly relationships, and with whom I would, more often than not, play the role of the therapist, but even these would, on occasion, discover some way to sabotage me in the hope of their own career advancement. The same was true of relatives and of people in general to whom I had shown much kindness.

I didn't seek revenge for the betrayals of these lesser beings, but instead became increasingly reclusive. When I was able to hold a job, which usually wasn't for very long, I performed my duties with excellence, but did so miserably, and took joy only in that which I could partake in outside of the workplace, activities which would commonly be considered as hobbies. Apart from the aforementioned creative pursuits I also held a great interest in the occult and was both a lifelong student and practitioner of the esoteric sciences. This interest was, admittedly, naturally endowed by such occurrences as visions and the like which were onset from a very young age.

In the midst of my influenza I had not left my home for a span of about two weeks. I probably would have seldom left my home anyway, for I was out of work and survived on account of some clever stock investments which I had secured which provided me with gradual growth and a healthy, albeit moderate, income of dividends. My needs were simple in any case.

During this two week span I entered into a perpetual state of what is commonly known as the "fever dream", throughout which I was subject to visions of a myriad sort. Recurring were the visitations to a type of other-dimensional biotechnology laboratory wherein I was offered a job of overseeing certain obscure mutational developments in humanoid subjects. I told my prospective other-dimensional employers, who appeared with grey skin, were abnormally long and lean and who were, physiologically, with illogical bone and joint structures, that I would consider their offer.

Then one day I awoke feeling quite fine. My strength and stamina were still not up to par but I no longer detected any sign of fever or omnipresent soreness like I had for some time. I decided that some fresh air would do me good and ventured by car to a nearby park which borders the ocean, thinking that the sea air would do me some good, its currents rising up from South America where, for the time being anyway, a vast amount of diverse oxygen-producing trees yet remained.

As I sat in my car with the driver-side window open (the other windows did not function) I put on some avant-garde jazz music and relaxed for awhile. On the way into the park I observed a missing-persons sign which depicted a young girl, perhaps of 15 or so, and gave a New Jersey phone number to call for any information concerning her whereabouts. I didn't initially think much of it, however I was prompted by something to turn and look at the sign again, which was placed at the edge of the parking lot, and was suddenly given a vision of the girl. I saw that she was in a poor state, filthy, evidently beaten and perhaps raped, seated in a dark space, perhaps a warehouse. I entered more deeply into the vision and was able to indicate the surrounding area, which I recognized as Newark, NJ.

I have often been prone to such visions and seldom act upon them in any way. It was commonly my fear that, apart from being faced with ridicule at suggesting I had the ability for remote-viewing, I could potentially be institutionalized. I have nothing but mistrust for the extroverted world, as has probably been suggested. What those people can do alone, or worse, in the midst of their groupthink, is simply appalling to think about. At best, in this type of scenario, I would have written a short semi-fictional story about it and left it at that.

In this instance however, and perhaps it was my semi-ill state that prompted me to it, or so I speculated, I experienced a rare moment of ambition. If I was indeed able to help locate this missing girl perhaps I could become something of a consultant for such cases. I was sure it would pay well, and could be, at the least, interesting, and more importantly, solitary work. I decided to call the number on the sign at that moment.

"Hello?" a female voice on the other end answered. "Hello, I am calling in regards to the disappearance of a girl, Linda Martinez if I am not mistaken. I believe I may have an idea of where she is." The recipient began to speak to someone else who was with them, although I couldn't make out what they said and assumed they were reiterating my statement. She then said "Oh my God, please, any help you have would be so appreciated." I told the woman, who revealed herself as Linda's mother, that I would like to meet in person to discuss the knowledge that I had and she agreed to this. She lived in East Brunswick, NJ and I made my way to her home that day. It was only about 30 minutes drive. I stopped for tea at a Starbucks along the way, utilizing the drive-through of course so as to minimize any social interaction. The barista was far too peppy to be genuine.

I rang the bell at the address I was given, an average middle-class suburban home, and the mother of Linda, a petite brunette, answered the door. She bore a striking resemblance to her daughter, unsurprisingly, and looked to have been in a state of perpetual tears and worry for some time. Her husband stood a little way behind her; he was a man of medium height, middle-aged, bald and of a moderately strong build. "How average all of this is", I remarked silently to myself before extending a hand in greeting to the mother and father. They invited me in and we sat at their kitchen table, I across from them.

"As I indicated to you earlier, I believe that I have information concerning the location of your daughter. She is alive, but is... otherwise in poor shape it would seem." The father spoke, "How did you get this information? Do you know our daughter?" This last statement was spoken with a look that resembled a combination of confusion and disgust; after all, why would his teenage daughter be associating with a 30 year old man? "No I have never met your daughter, nor known of her existence until I happened upon her missing-persons sign today. The source of my information is... well... psychic, I suppose you may say." A fallen look came over the faces of the parents. "It is up to you to consider or dismiss the information I have collected. I offer it freely, however I would like a favor in return. If my information is accurate I would like you to attest to it before any involved law enforcement agencies."

The couple looked at each other in a puzzled way then turned to me. The mother said, "What do you know?" I nodded and proceeded, "She is being held in Newark, NJ against her will, or so I suspect given the state that I saw her in. As for the specific location, it is a dark storage area, perhaps a warehouse. I will have to be closer to her proximity to disclose the precise location, but am quite confident that, once in Newark, we will be able to find her promptly. Needless to say, we should inform the police about this and get moving as soon as possible." In truth, I had never done anything like this before, but felt a sense of trust in my abilities nonetheless. There was some semblance of a guiding hand in all of this which I did not quite comprehend, but in which I felt a strange sense of assurance.

Perhaps two hours later I was with Linda's parents, two detectives and two police officers in Newark. It did not take me long to discover the location we were seeking, although it came as a surprise to me that it was in a storage unit center. The police were sent into the main office by the detectives (I suppose this was a hierarchical procedure) to notify them that we required admittance to the premises and a few moments later we stood in the midst of hundreds of storage units of varying sizes. I separated myself from the group, who walked a little way behind me, and paced along aisles of steel doors until involuntarily stopping in front of one indoor unit. The hallway was dimly lit and featured concrete floors, walls and ceilings. Shadows played in the dark spaces where the warm-colored lights did not quite reach.

"Unit 269" I said aloud with a note of solemn confidence, as though I was taking part in some David Lynch production. The office worker employed the use of a bolt cutter to break the lock and proceeded to open the vertical steel door. The mother let out a scream, one of the detectives voiced an obscenity, and I held no particularly strong reaction save for surprise. Linda was indeed in this otherwise empty unit, although not quite in the manner which my vision had showed me. Hooks had been drilled into the concrete walls of the unit, upon which were fastened chains which bound the girl in a standing position. From the waist down she had been sawn in half. Her entrails and the lower part of her body were strung about the room. The smell was that of decay; I suspected that she had been this way for several days. Her face had the colors of a putrid green and black, colors which I hoped I could incorporate into some future artwork.

The forensics team arrived shortly afterwards as did an FBI agent who, I thought, looked the part in a rather cliche manner. I was questioned by the agent, as well as the detectives, as to how I had obtained the location of the missing girl. The agent seemed less surprised by my methods than did the detectives. It suddenly occurred to me at that moment that I could potentially be held as a person of suspicion about all of this, a factor which I had strangely neglected to consider up to that point. Thankfully this did not seem to be the case.

The forensics team were unable to discover any fingerprints whatsoever, and a few days later I was informed by the detectives that the only DNA, apart from Linda's, that was found belonged, strangely, to a type of cephalopod. As the FBI agent was making his leave I took the opportunity to catch up to him and present myself as a potential asset to help in cases such as this. "We have our people for that type of thing" he said cooly and dismissively before walking off. So much for my ambitious idea, or so I thought.

I was asked by the detectives to come back to the police station and did so, not that I had a choice as I had commuted with them. Linda's parents were in a terrible state and I felt rather awkward sitting next to them in the back of the detective car. I kept my attention facing out of the window. When we arrived at the police station I was led into the office of one of the detectives and asked to sign some paperwork which accounted for my personal information. I was also fingerprinted as a precaution, per their request. Then one of the detectives, Jacobson was his surname, produced a file from within his desk and tossed it in front of me. He made a hand gesture for me to examine it and I opened it. Inside was a stack of missing-persons papers. All of them were, invariably, young girls, mostly between the age of 10-15. According to the documentation some had been missing for quite some time, but one in particular, who had disappeared only a week previously, caught my eye.

"Natalia Lisovetsky" I said aloud in a low voice. The detective eyed me strangely. "That girl just went missing last week. If I'm not mistaken, she and her family are from your neck of the woods." Strange, I thought. I closed my eyes for a moment and the visions came rapidly again. This time they were more gruesome than the last. I suppose my mental filter had, since seeing the mutilated corpse of Linda, become more brutally honest in that short span of time. Furthermore, I could identify the precise location immediately, perhaps due to my relative familiarity with it. "I know where she is," I stated firmly to Detective Jacobson.

As you might imagine I was becoming relatively impressed with myself at this point. The possibility of solving two missing-persons cases in one day was a rare feat. The location where my vision had showed me this girl was but ten minutes or so from my home, on the south shore of Staten Island, NY. It was outside of the jurisdiction of the New Jersey police but Detective Jacobson made a call to 123 New York City police precinct and I agreed to meet with the police officers at that location. Before departing, Detective Jacobson shook my hand and said, "I don't know how you're able to do what you do, and if I'm honest I feel conflicted about it, but you have some type of gift and we are lucky that you are using it for the right reasons."

When I arrived to the 123 precinct on Main Street I informed the desk officer of my reason for being there; this was after the officer altogether ignored my presence for about seven minutes or so and continued to process his paperwork, feigning obliviousness to my arrival. He told me to have a seat and continued his paperwork for a few moments before disappearing through a door and returning to his work a few moments later. Two youngish police officers exited through a door that led into the waiting area and approached me. "You the psychic?" one of them asked with a cynical tone. "That's me", I said.

I was escorted to the back of their patrol car and directed them to the location in which my vision had showed me the missing girl. It was only about a mile away, in a warehouse district that bordered the nearby harbor. On the way one of the officers said to me, "If you really do have visions it must be an act of God." I remarked to him that I didn't believe in any higher power, and he shrugged. I recognized the fish wholesaler, Shelly's Seafood, as we approached it, and pointed for them that this was the location. They shook their heads and pulled into the small parking lot. Shelly's Seafood was closed at this time of the evening. It was a moderately sized blue warehouse with a shipment bay at the front. "The girl is in this place?" one of the officers asked. I looked at the warehouse for a moment, and said "No... she is near though. Let's take a look around the property."

We made our way around the back of the unkempt grounds of the property which were thick with brush. Amidst large and reeking dumpsters there was an old storage shed. "In there" I told the officers. With flashlight in hand, one of the officers slowly approached the shed while the other produced his handgun and kept it trained on the door. The officer opened the shed, which was unlocked, and involuntarily began to vomit. Inside the small space, which was lit by a single hanging lightbulb without a lamp, were strewn human remains. If these were the remains of the girl in question it was difficult to tell, save for a small and filthy foot which had been tossed carelessly on the floor. The remainder had been, seemingly, pulverized. The scent was wretched, although not much worse, I remarked to myself, than the rotting fish in the nearby dumpsters.

It was likely the psychological impact which caused the officer to vomit. As for myself, I took care to observe the strange textures of the bloody pulp of a mess, again to incorporate into some future artworks. If nothing else, this day had been a source of great creative inspiration for me.

Detectives arrived shortly after and I was brought back to the station for questioning, to fill out paperwork, fingerprinting and the same bureaucratic process that I had already been treated to earlier that day. They told me they would keep in touch, and I took my leave to go home, which was a few minutes drive.

By this point I was quite exhausted and, as I had mentioned earlier, was still recovering from the influenza. I took the opportunity to hydrate, fed my cats and went to sleep. On the verge of entering sleep I slipped into the hypnagogic state, as is often the case for me, and beheld strange visions.

There was a type of cult who met, and seemingly lived, in an abandoned network of buildings that I did not recognize. They wore dark robes imprinted with strange insignia and in the midst of their occult workings was ever an eerie green luminescence, which was almost akin to a negative light or color. I saw that their workings induced a state of hypnosis into unsuspecting people; specifically I watched as they extended this influence unto various young girls in the midst of their sleep. The girls, once awakening from their slumber, would be in a state of deep trance in which they would venture to specific locations which were pre-coordinated for them. Once there, one or more of the cultists would proceed to torture and mutilate the girls. Throughout these acts it was observed that a type of energetic essence was released into the atmosphere, and as I watched this occur a multitude of times I saw that the same negative coloration was gradually enveloping the world. I saw that similar cults were performing an identical set of operations throughout the earth, operating as they did in isolated cell units at the fringes of human civilization, and entirely unknown to it.

A truly strange element of these visions was that the young girls, rather than expressing horror of pain in the midst of their torture and murder, seemed in nearly all instances to be entirely indifferent to it. A few of them even smiled, and one laughed with a sinister howl.

At the conclusion of these visions I myself stood amidst the cultists, rather than as a bodiless observer from a distance as had been the case up to that point. At first it did not appear that they took notice of me, but then one of them approached me directly and, holding a hot iron brand, imprinted on my forehead a peculiar symbol which resembled a many-appendaged form.

For the remainder of the night I entered a dreamless black sleep, or so was all that I recalled, though I suspect that there was much more to it which I was not then prepared to process.

Part 2

I awoke the next morning feeling more or less fine. I would still require a couple of more days to heal completely from my influenza, and I was sure that the lack of rest on the previous day would not have helped this process, but I felt myself to be in a pleasant mood overall, inasmuch as my moods could be described as pleasant. I decided to go out for a cup of coffee, something I hadn't indulged in for several weeks at this point, in part because of the flu, and in part because the particular form of caffeine derived from coffee does not compliment my sensitive heart.

When I opened my front door I saw that an unassuming envelope had been placed at the foot of it. I picked up the envelope, which had not been sealed shut. There were no markings of any kind written upon it. Inside the envelope was a piece of strange parchment, perhaps made of hemp, upon which was a symbol which I then recognized as the same one from my hypnagogic visions of the previous night. I had all but forgotten about those visions prior to this point. A cold chill swept through me and there was a feeling of bleakness which was only worsened when I produced the only other contents of the envelope, a photo of a completely robed individual assuming an occult posture called "the Sign of Silence".

Just then my phone rang and I answered it despite not recognizing the number. It was an officer from the 123 precinct. They informed me that during the previous night they were notified of four more missing girls.

They wanted me to come in to act as a consultant with them, and even offered to hire me as an independent contractor. We would go over the details of everything when I arrived, they assured me.

This was unexpected good news and I was quite happy with myself about it. But then I suppose it was my mistake to neglect the intelligence and security of my general pessimistic outlook as concerns humanity. The situation was, of course, too good to be true.

When I arrived at the police station two officers immediately seized me, and brought me to a holding cell. Along the way they explained that I was under arrest and read me my Miranda rights. I was pushed into a cell rather carelessly and found that my cellmate was an old homeless drunkard who was passed out. I suspected, correctly as it would turn out, that I had been placed under arrest as a suspect for various kidnappings and murders such as those which I had aided the police in discovering.

As I awaited my fate in the filthy cell I entered a state of reflection (to be honest, when wasn't I in a state of reflection? Such is the curse of being self-aware, a quality which is possessed by very few) and noted with a pessimistic irony that it really doesn't pay to be altruistic, least of all to be ambitious. Initially, I was not entirely sure what the motivating factor behind my behavior in this instance was. Decidedly it was the mistake, however uncommon for me, of acting with ambition, that would lead to my demise. As I have stated, this world is simply not designed for the introverted types. Rather, it seems designed to punish genuine intelligence and introspection with poverty, existential dread and, in this instance, incarceration.

My internal monologue was interrupted by the rousing awake of the drunken derelict I had noted earlier. This should be interesting, I thought, although it far exceeded my expectations. The man initially sat upright and seemed in a sleepy daze, then looked with his terrible blue eyes into my own. I have always, I should note, found that a certain mania tends to exist in those humans who are with blue eyes. They seem always with a particular tendency to force themselves onto the world, as though that color is with some electrifying quality.

The derelict spoke with a truly surprising sense of clarity. "Have you discovered the Green Harlequin? It looks like this." He unbuttoned his flannel shirt at the top and held it open, bearing a scarred chest, the center of which bore the same sign that I had seen twice thus far; once in my vision and once in the obscure envelope that was left at my door. I didn't respond to him.

"The threshold is loosening boy." He continued, "You have your part to play too. All of us do. Most never realize it, never take notice of those who pull the strings. But I can see it in your eyes, you've witnessed it, you've contemplated it. That's why they chose you." He gave a sick smile that revealed vile and jagged teeth, and didn't speak again after this. Nor did I have an opportunity to question him further, as he very suddenly began to have a seizure, with eerie smile intact, then grabbed the bars of the cell and smashed his head into them until it was a bloody mess. I didn't bother to try and stop him; he was even more filthy than the cell after all, perhaps diseased, and I didn't want to touch him.

Some police officers eventually came to check on the commotion. They hadn't been in any rush, and I was able to hear them making meaningless small-talk some distance away all throughout this incident. When they arrived to my cell they drew their handguns and cuffed me. It was assumed, based upon the reason for my arrest and their false presumptions, that I had murdered the derelict in question. I spent the remainder of the day in another, solitary, cell, cuffed and rather uncomfortable. I found the handcuffs to be overkill. A detective, beige trenchcoat and all, whose name I do not recall came to visit me a while later after forensics had examined the corpse of the derelict.

"What is the deal with the cephalopods?" he asked rather casually. "Excuse me?", I responded. "This is the third incident in which a corpse was found in relation to yourself, and in all three instances

forensics discovered cephalopod DNA. Truth be told, I am flabbergasted as to how you managed it inside of that cell." Obviously I was just as confused as he was about this matter. I shrugged and didn't say a word, assuming at this point that any further dialogue would only incriminate me. After a few moments the detective sighed, mumbled something under his breath and walked away.

At some point in the middle of the night two officers came and told me I was being transferred. They wouldn't explain why, but I surmised it was because I was, at this point, considered to be too violent for a holding cell. Maybe it was simply part of their bureaucratic process, I am not sure. We followed Arthur Kill Rd about ten minutes to the high security prison which seemed so out of place on Staten Island. I won't bore you with the details of my processing, but after a few hours in the doldrums I was escorted by prison guards to my solitary cell. There was a positive side to all of this after all; at least I wouldn't have to share a cell.

It was about dawn by this time and I wasn't sure how long I would have to sleep before I was awakened, presumably by some type of alarm, so I layed in the bed which was not quite long enough for my height and entered into a type of meditative trance that I found to be relatively rejuvenating. An hour or so later a loud, building-wide alarm resonated and roused me out of my trance. Nothing in particular happened for a little while, and then my door unlocked and opened. I crept, somewhat unwillingly, toward the open door and saw that amidst several guards in the hallway the other prisoners were making their way to a doorway. One of the guards saw me looking puzzled and told me to "come on", so I did.

We, though I hate to use that word and associate myself with those delinquents, were herded to an open cafeteria for breakfast. I seized up the room and noted that segregation was alive and well within these prison walls; the prisoners appeared to be secluded almost exclusively into racial groups, though occasionally mixed-racial groups existed where some particularly orthodox religion was practiced by them. There were many Muslims, I noted.

I received my breakfast which consisted primarily of carb-heavy foods that I usually avoided and was set to the task of finding a place to eat. The neo-nazis? No, despite the color of my skin my dark eyes would give away my mixed racial ancestry. The Italians? No, I had had enough of gangsters, having grown up around many of them. None of the options really looked promising, and there were language barriers amidst many groups, I noted while walking around. I finally settled upon what seemed to be the table of outcasts, a mixed bag of weirdos, probably pedophiles I thought, who at least seemed quiet enough. The other inmates seemed to avoid walking near this group as well, and I figured maybe they could offer some type of protection in this hellhole.

I sat down at their table with some hesitation. The lot of them, there were seven, all turned a rather empty gaze toward me as I eyed each of them in turn, then began to pick at my food. I didn't have much of an appetite, truth be told. One of them, a scrawny man with a shaved head, perhaps around my age, addressed me first without looking up. "Quite a mess with little Linda wasn't it?", he said in a softly spoken voice. Had the circumstances leading to this moment not been so obscure, perhaps I would have been surprised. I didn't reply to him nonetheless, as had become my chosen method of communication, or non-communication as it were.

Another of the group continued where he left off, "And Natalia. She was a sweet one." A third went on, "Humanity really is a pitiful species. The best it can hope for is its own extinction. Wouldn't you agree?" I thought for a moment and said, simply, "Yes, I suppose that is true." The third man continued, "To place an innocent man into a place like this with the scum of the earth, all because he was trying to be helpful, it is truly a vile thing. Worry not my new friend, preparations are in motion, and this moment of discomfort will be but a fleeting one."

I wasn't quite sure what he meant by that last statement but I didn't ask, and the remainder of our meal was eaten in silence, which was fine with me. Following this I was escorted back to my solitary cell. My lunch and dinner were brought to me directly; apparently this was a type of semi-solitary confinement. I didn't mind it and spent the day in self-analysis, having assumed a basically stoic attitude toward the situation.

I drifted to sleep at some point in the evening but was awakened by a commotion. Sleep was going to be difficult in this place, I thought. Then the door to my cell clicked and opened. Outside the other prisoners stepped into the hall, looking confused, and the commotion that had awakened me was heard coming from the cafeteria. I ventured in that direction and saw that a riot had broken out. It was, to quote Anthony Burgess, a state of ultraviolence that I beared witness to here. Prisoners were viciously attacking other prisoners, prisoners and guards were attacking one another, even guards were attacking other guards. It was chaos. I felt no particular motivation to join in with it, and nobody seemed to take notice of me as I casually walked through the chaos toward my breakfast-mates. "It is time." said the third man from earlier, and the eight of us made our way, entirely without incident, through a maze of hallways and open doors to exit the prison.

The fresh air outside was a welcome change to the stuffiness within the prison walls and we commandeered two police vehicles outside. I wasn't asked to drive and took my seat in the back of one of them. Not a word was spoken as we made our way to a deeply wooded area of the island which was very close to its center. We parked near what I recognized as the abandoned psychiatric center, a massive facility which was located within a large acreage of forested land, and around which was a high fence at all perimeters. We exited our cars and I followed the others to a place in the steel fence where a large hole had been cut. We climbed through with ease and they lead the way toward the complex of abandoned and decrepit buildings which once served as a place for dark experiments to be performed upon myriad an unwilling patient.

Staten Island had a very dark history which most of its inhabitants remained, and would forever remain, entirely unaware of. I had mused previously upon the fact that this location was at the dead center of the island, and had even visited it once with some friends while in high school. Many people who visited this place reported a sinister presence and certain visions, such as a black dog, which were consistently perceived amongst many visitors. I had seen that apparition myself during my previous visit to this place.

My reflections were interrupted by our arrival to the massive central building which featured a monolithic cement ramp that extended to the second floor from outside. We ascended the ramp and entered the large entrance room, where I saw, and I suppose I may as well have seen this coming, a group of figures robed entirely in black. My companions obtained robes from a corner where they formed a pile and one of the figures, who seemed to be female, brought me one as well. I undressed and put the robe on, as seemed to be the custom.

A robed woman spoke, "The final sacrifice for our part will arrive soon." and with that all of the cultists formed a semicircle around a rusty old hospital bed, the arrangement of which I joined them in. For a moment I contemplated whether, and at this point it wouldn't have surprised me, I myself was to be the sacrifice that was indicated, but this thought was dismissed a few moments later as a young girl, perhaps 11 years old, entered the building. She was clearly hypnotically entranced. Two of the cultists approached her, took her by the hand on either side, and walked her over to the hospital bed. They undressed and then lifted the girl onto the bed, utilizing restraints to extend her small limbs openly in the shape of an X.

Another cultist stepped forward from our semi-circular arrangement (there did not appear to be any particular type of hierarchy here, I noted, but rather a communistic sense of "from each according to his ability") and produced a wand like object which appeared to be constructed of copper or brass, though it was difficult to tell in this environment which was illuminated only marginally by moonlight and a few candles. This figure made his way to the entranced girl and held the wand-like object out before her. She had no particular response and simply stared out blankly. The congregation began to chant a type of incantation, which went "A'agash Chava Raflo'q Ta'ava Ma'alugkh". The cultist with the wand gradually lowered it and began to caress the thighs of the girl with it before caressing her vulva with the same, and suddenly penetrating it, at which time the chanting grew louder. I had joined in with the chanting at this point, and was entering a type of trance myself.

A putrid green light began to subtly fill the atmosphere, increasing in density as we chanted and as this strange ritual commenced. The wand was removed from the vulva of the girl and the blood of her broken hymen was employed as paint, with which the cultist in question proceeded to draw the same symbol, evidently the sign of the Green Harlequin, upon her naked chest. The top half of the wand was then pulled off, revealing a wickedly sharp blade which glistened in the partial light and green luminescence alike, and the cultists drove the blade into the center of the symbol before dragging it down her torso, effectively ripping open this entire part of her body. The entire congregation now rushed forward in a state of mania, and I included in their ranks, as we proceeded to rip the body of the girl apart and devour whatever organs we could grasp at in a frenzy of blood and ecstasy.

After a time a cultist near me grabbed my arm and motioned for me to join a few of the others who were collecting pieces of wood and accumulating them into a pile at the opposite end of the large space. Another cultist doused these in a liquid, presumably gasoline, and placed one of the candles into it. Another group of cultists carried the bed which held the girl to the fire, once it was sufficiently large, and placed it, mattress down, onto the flame. The eerie green luminescence was now so bright that it illuminated the dark hall and from the smoke of the fire it took the form of a deep fog, which filled the hall and extended out of every broken window and doorway into the outer world. Our entire congregation stepped outside and watched as the green fog extended in all directions, filling the forest and sky alike. I myself stepped before our congregation and exclaimed, in a state of bloodlusting mania, "The threshold has been broken!"

Part 3

In the following weeks the human species entered into a state of absolute pandemonium. The last threads which held humanity from the brink of the abyss had snapped. What began as a sudden outbreak of violent racial conflicts and random murders rapidly escalated into nuclear war between all nations. It was not just our cell of cultists, but cells like it all throughout the earth which had been preparing this operation for some time. We operated unbeknownst to one another yet in perfect synchronicity, driven as we were by an unseen agency.

Our congregation was not immune to the mass-extinction which had become imminent. We dispersed following the sacrificial ritual previously described, but I can only assume that they, like myself, perished in the nuclear fire.

At the point of my death I did not immediately enter a state of absolute blackness and nothingness, although by the time you read these passages I am assured that I will have attained to that state of perfect eternal sleep. Instead, with death my consciousness, though I no longer feel the term "my" to have ever been applicable, entered a strange other-dimensional state of being in which I drifted amidst the most brilliant colors I had ever witnessed. I was approached in this state by a group of cephalopod-like creatures which nonetheless only retained a biological at times, and at others seemed something else entirely, like a raw expression of quantum foam. They were, nonetheless, immensely beautiful and horrifying in similitude. Their forms sometimes appeared before me, and at other times seemed to stretch across the entirety of infinity and seemed as though they were on the verge of being ripped apart, an event which, it seemed, would collapse the entire universal matrix; they seemed to gain a sense of what may be considered arousal by such a prospect, and maintained themselves in turn upon that threshold of annihilation in the manner of an eternally prolonged near-orgasm.

They communicated to me in what may be described, for your benefit, as a telepathic manner, although I realized then that they and I were in truth one in the same; I was but one of their appendages all along, as all of us are. My instruction, accomplishable only from my present vantage point, was to deliver this story to an unwitting individual of a certain time, one whose mind was sufficiently numb to the world so as to be capable of receiving it in its entirety. Thus it is that you were chosen to record this testament, unbeknownst to you, that the hopelessness of the human species may be revealed to the world by your medium and advocacy. It is time that you and I separate, for, as I have indicated, there are greater aspirations for myself, but rest assured that yours will be the same fate as my own.

The Star

The following is the transcript of an obscure suicide note that I received from an acquantence of mine. At his request, I am publishing it within this volume of short stories, as I believe it fits the general themes which I myself describe in the midst of these short stories. As for my friend, he was notoriously a recluse, but we maintained communication through electronic means for many years until such a time when his reclusive nature isolated him totally, as I am told from others who knew him, from the remainder of humanity. It is my sincere hope that he found what he was looking for.

I tend to avoid the consumption of media by all costs. I couldn't care less about what is going on in the world at large, if I am honest. Wars, politics, business, culture; I feel completely isolated from all of these things. For the most part I remain a recluse, lest I expose myself to the idiotic meanderings of other humans. I am loathe to even consider myself of the same species as those other creatures, and have always felt myself to be different from the remainder of them, if only because I am so uncompromisingly myself in an individual way.

Research is, however, another matter altogether. I enjoy researching the history and development of the human species and do so quite frequently. I seem to be searching for something but admit to being unsure as to precisely what this is. If nothing else, I have gained great insight into human nature as an unchanging phenomenon since prehistory; the tools and technologies change but the behaviors remain the same. Such is yet another reason that I avoid media at all costs. It is little more than a broadcasting device intended to program and reprogram the antennae which comprise the minds of unsuspecting idiots. But I digress from this point.

It was in the midst of my research into, of all things, Japanese New Religious Movements that I discovered the Happiness Movement. It was a cult of course, like all religious movements, but was relatively unique in terms of its wide scale global success. With a little research I was surprised to discover that it maintained branches close to my proximity of residence.

I have always been intrigued by the Japanese creative aesthetic. I may abhor media as pertains to worldly affairs, but I enjoy genuine creative endeavors in the manner of film, music, artworks and so forth. Naturally there is a division to be made between genuine works and those produced purely for commercial and cultural broadcasting purposes. To be safe, I restrict my intake of such things to those works which treat of topics such as nihilism, misanthropy, cosmicism, existential dread, the occult, and horror in general. Japan produces many such works and does so with excellence, so I had by this time, over a course of many years, familiarized myself with many Japanese creative endeavors.

So it was that, out of curiosity more than anything, I decided to contact the Happiness Movement and inquire about visiting one of their temples. This decision was made following my watching a few of the movies they produced and reading a few of the books written by their leader, a man who claims (don't they all) to be the reincarnation of the Buddha Shakyamuni as well the only living incarnation of the god that oversees and rules this earth and planetary system. On this last point, the Happiness Movement was always a little bit hazy; sometimes the leader in question, who was referred to as Master Ryu, claimed he was the incarnation of God altogether, while at other times he was simply the god of the earth, or else of the central sun of this solar system. It seemed an intentionally confusing affair, as is often the case with cults, as the constant state of disinformation keeps members in a state of confusion and unknowing, and accordingly, dependence upon the chain of information that the cult provides.

The man I contacted in the Happiness Movement, via email, stated that he was a minister and that he would be very happy (of course) for me to come and visit. He inquired further about my interest in and familiarity with the movement, which I informed him about. A week later I made my way to one of their branches, which I had some little difficulty locating as it was nested within a multi-use office building in an obscure location bordering a river.

Once inside the building I immediately spotted the Happiness Movement plaque above the door to their suite and walked in, noting the free pamphlets and magazines of their movement near the entrance. Following a long hallway I entered into what seemed to be a bookstore that housed at least a thousand different books, many of which were written in Japanese. This Ryu character certainly had a knack for writing, I thought. There was nobody in this room but I quickly found them in another room around the corner. They were exclusively Japanese and were, without exception, immensely welcoming and polite. The man whom I had contacted introduced himself and stated that he was happy (big surprise) to meet me. I sat down at a table, noting that the room had been arranged with tables and chairs facing forward to a nicely designed altar, upon which were a cadeuscus wand and dagger, and behind which was an alcove which displayed a golden mandala.

The people around me, all quite friendly, began to inquire with me about how I discovered the Happiness Movement. I discussed my comparative-religious studies and they were all apparently very impressed.

Truth be told, they were probably the nicest group of people I have ever met. I felt, and it was a rare thing, genuinely comfortable and at ease around them. When they began to refer to the leader of the movement as Master Ryu, and when the man with whom I initially spoke referred to this Master Ryu as a god in the flesh, I naturally reminded myself that this was, after all, a cult, but outwardly I went along with it all.

There was a brief lecture following our introductions and at the end of it I inquired about becoming a member, which required only a small donation. I agreed to this and a small initiation ritual was conducted in which I took the three refuges of Buddhism, something which I had done before during a Tibetan Vajrayana Buddhist initiation. I was no stranger to the occult, far from it in fact. This made me all the more suspicious, as initiation ceremonies were usually only conducted after a period of necessary study and, at times, ordeals. I was given some books free of charge and made my departure after saying goodbye to everyone and, in a gesture that may or may not have been foolish, giving them a customary bow. During my drive home I felt surprisingly refreshed by the experience and was in an unusually optimistic mood; such was in contrast to my usual state of pessimism. It was nice to meet nice people though, even if they were all brainwashed. Some of them were second generation members, and many of them were elderly, a point I found fascinating as many cults tend to attract a younger audience, or so I believed at the time.

Following my initiation into the Happiness Movement I conducted a bit of research into the movement itself in order to try and find any criminalizing evidence of cult activity. All journalists who penetrated the movement were in agreement that it was indeed a cult on the grounds that the leader was basically worshipped, but I was unable to discover anything beyond that fact which was out of the ordinary. There were no accounts of sexual misconduct, no stalking, no violence, no communes. I wasn't quite disappointed, but was nonetheless with mixed feelings, as I felt that something was not entirely right with the movement in question.

Several days later I began to receive emails from members of the movement. These would continue in the ensuing weeks and though they initially were friendly greetings and sharing of information about the teachings, they gradually took on a rather insistent missionary tone. It was recommended me to take part in a training course, to join their book club, to visit their other temples, to travel to Japan and visit the larger temples. My usual response to such barrating requests is to simply disappear from the people making them and ignore them altogether; eventually most people get the hint, and if not I simply block any and all means of communication that they have with me. But with the Happiness Movement it was a little different; they were all so nice, polite, accommodating and, well, happy. I couldn't necessarily fault them for their hospitality and enthusiasm could I? No, I decided for some reason. Perhaps the brainwashing was setting in despite my every caution against it?

I decided to conduct some further research into this Master Ryu. Internet-based research wouldn't quite cut it, so I chose to employ another method. I performed a banishing ritual which serves the function not of banishing external things, but of internal interruptions. I sat, closed my eyes and exited my body onto the astral plane. I concentrated upon Ryu and located his energetic signature in Tokyo, and was likewise immediately transported to a place close to him. He was in a lavish house, which could more properly be called a fortress, around which was a large stone wall. Seated around him in what appeared to be a study room were several of his students, one of which was acting as a scribe for his dictations. Such was the manner in which he was able to write so many books, I noted. I reflected that if I had a scribe to record my monologues I would probably have thousands of books written as well by this time.

I positioned myself in the room and concentrated deeply upon the man Ryu, who was in fact with a brilliant golden glow that I had sensed and perceived amongst everything associated with the Happiness Movement. I perceived in this state of more deeply entranced vision that Ryu was in fact a direct incarnation of the central sun of this solar system, a direct agent for it sent here with a specific purpose. So far, so good, if not surprising considering the amount of self-proclaimed gods in the flesh throughout the world.

What I discovered next was something exceedingly sinister, however.

The agenda behind why the spirit of this particular star had sent a direct emissary to this planet was revealed to me as only a small component of a much broader dynamic. The earth, I came to understand, had at some point in history become converted into a type of farm for souls. I had previously been undecided as to the nature of what a "soul" was precisely, but I now saw that it was more appropriate called a "sol", a sun or a star. Each and every human was the incarnation of a particular star in the universe. Stars assumed incarnations upon various planetary bodies throughout the universe in order to learn about and experience the universe in a multitude of forms.

The reason that the global human population was increasing at such exponential rates was due to the earth having been converted by the spirit of its central sun into a type of trap for souls. It sent out something that amounted to a distress beacon throughout the galaxy, requesting the aid of other stars, but once a star took incarnation here it would become subject to a repetitive cycle of incarnations upon this planet.

The process was gradual at first but as technological developments were increasingly dreamed up by the spirit of the central sun behind Ryu the incarnate stars in question were better able to survive and repopulate. Each instance of reproduction opened a gateway to outer space and drew in the essence of another star.

This had the effect of creating a mechanical farming sequence by which new stellar incarnates would be born each day without any knowledge of the fact.

Once incarnate, the souls in question would live out their lives meaninglessly upon this planet and eventually die, however at the time of death they would be processed through yet another mechanism of reincarnation into the same exact system. All of this was with the purpose of biding the time until the eventual extinction of the human species, at which point the central sun of this solar system would absorb the essence of the stars which had incarnated into it. It was nothing less than a case of cosmic parasitism, and a highly successful one at that!

I departed the home of Ryu feeling considerably shaken at all that I had discovered and promptly returned to my physical body. I sat in a meditative state for awhile and then endeavored to communicate with my own star, what may be considered my higher self. These words were spoken to me:

"In order to free yourself from this world you must do what you were sent here to do, which is to create. In the world you presently reside within it is the artists and musicians who are able, if they pursue these practices with care, to create the conditions for the planetary systems that surround their own star. Make use of this, design the reality that I have willed for you to design. Then, when you are ready, hold my image and the image of your world in mind, and depart the vessel which has parasitically contained you for so long."

I was also informed of how I would come to identify my own star, and eventually did, but I will refrain from including the name it is known by on earth for reasons of privacy. I will, however, describe the manner in which I would come to discover it.

I cut all communication with the Happiness Movement following this experience and placed the whole of my efforts instead upon fulfilling the instructions that had been communicated to me. I became increasingly reclusive, more than I had ever been, and converted my home into an art studio at every capacity. I made use of my multi-instrumentalism to compose and record music which was entirely unearthly, the sounds of my own world which conveyed the feelings of the same. I painted majestically strange landscapes and creatures until every surface of my home was covered with them, all the while set to the strange music that I had created.

Throughout this work, which lasted several years, I kept current with astronomical news and research as I was instructed to do. Incredibly, a concentration had been made upon a particular planet in another solar system upon which life had seemingly begun to emerge. Telescopic evidence revealed what appeared to be signs of advanced civilization upon the planet in question, and then upon other planets surrounding it. Radio signal receivers likewise transmitted various strange signals from the planetary system in question, signals which were unlike any received from the remainder of the universe. I came to realize that the uproar in the astronomy community was about me, about my own higher self. Humanity is a very long way from being able to travel to my own stellar system, thankfully, and I suspect they will have become extinct long before they have created the opportunity for interstellar travel.

When at last my creative work was done, and having identified with precision the location and nature of my own star, I decided to record all of this as a final testament. I have gifted it to an acquaintance for publishing. By the time it is in your hands I will have released myself from my mortal vessel and from this prison, and will have returned to the place where I belong. I wish that is received well, and may inspire you, whomever you are, toward the willful return to your own unique star.

Euthanasia

Existence within the ontology of a city environment is enough to incite homicidal thoughts and acts. I was not immune to this and, far from being exempt, was at the forefront of constructing an exceedingly violent imagination. Such was the only thing that provided me with any semblance of solace in the midst of my daily affairs, which took place in a claustrophobic context at nearly all times. The simplest of activities all entailed stepping amidst a great and dull mass of collective human filth which in every way appeared to move through the world in the least sensible manner possible and was with a seemingly omnipresent malevolence.

I had not always resided in the "city that never sleeps" (and how I wish it would, permanently!); by contrast, there was a time where I had escaped my place of birth for a span of years and retreated into the mountains up north. Those were wonderful years spent in peace and quiet, amidst fresh air and the sounds of nature. I remember well the howling of coyotes, which is the most hauntingly beautiful sound I have ever listened to. How I longed for my isolated cabin, nested as it was in a place which even the locals of that region referred to as "God's country" on account of its isolation and high altitude.

I held a simple job there and though the money was not much when compared to the standards of the city it was enough to sustain me. My wife likewise held a simple job there, and between the two of us, due to our uncommonly educated nature for that region, our own household income was double the average for the region.

It was her parents, the wretched creatures, who, in the midst of their monthly visit, were ever insistent that we had no future there. Such insistence, I am quite ashamed to admit, eventually wore away at me over the course of several years. More so than that, it was the complexities of office politics and in particular the sharing of an office with one particular woman that catalyzed my eventual departure from paradise.

Patricia was her name. She was middle-aged and had finagled a situation in which she was able to work the same job as I on a per diem basis so that she came and went as she pleased. Most days she would arrive at the office, located within a non-profit habilitation center for individuals with developmental disabilities, sometime between 10-11am. Always she wore the same fake smile, bearing a full set of large teeth like an enraged chimpanzee.

The vile woman Patricia, who sat but five feet away from me in this office space, had managed to become the vizier of our new supervisor, a stupid girl several years younger than myself who lacked both the intellect and the compassion to be working in such a place. Patricia claimed that she was an anarchist at heart and before I transferred from the accounting department I believed her to be a nice enough woman with whom I shared some occasionally stimulating conversations. What I came to discover was that, for an anarchist, she was positively obsessed with bureaucracy and law. Without diving into unnecessary details, she was militantly insistent upon promoting her ideal of increased regulation for our company-wide recording procedures, something which the unique position we shared in the company could allow us some fair say in. Not only was her ideal rationally unnecessary but it would account for an increase of tedious work not just for myself and our other office mate, who was quite a nice girl that shared my own sentiments about the situation, but would likewise affect the workload of hundreds of already disgruntled and underpaid employees.

As I have inferred, she had caught the ear of our young, stupid and impressionable supervisor who idealized, but didn't know the first thing about altruism, and believed that Patricia's agenda was for the "greater good". I imagined daily murdering both of these women in the most gruesome ways possible.

It was that situation, coupled with the vile thought-seed which had been planted by my in-laws, which eventually compelled me to suggest to my wife that we relocate back to the pit of hell in which we had been born. My wife was against the idea but I somehow persuaded her that it was for the best, and had been persuaded myself by forces which can only be a source of genuine malice. We made our plans for departure and a short time later took to temporarily residing with my in-laws in a spare bedroom of theirs.

I had been assured, and reassured, that there was a great abundance of high-paying jobs available in the city. Well, it had been two years and apart from some occasional freelance work I had been unemployed. The problem was that, sure, there were plenty of jobs, but also an overabundance of humans applying to them! I would not even state that the fair majority of these jobs were high-paying, and most were sparsely above the minimum wage. I had been duped, and worse still, my wife and I were steeped in a state of misery due to our environmental conditions which were unsuitable to us. It was all we could do to reminisce about the paradise that we had willfully left behind, and we lived in a perpetual state of regret concerning this fact.

Within the hell of the city, my in-laws, along with their vile little dog, a maltese-yorkie chimera, played the role of the demons whose business was to serve as a constant reminder of the hell we resided in. It wasn't so bad at first as both of them worked and the dog was quiet so long as my mother-in-law wasn't around her. Once they both retired, only a short time after we had relocated there, it became genuine hell on earth. They were simply always there, always loud, and that horrible dog was always barking.

My in-laws, I may as well explain, were both immigrants from Italy. Though they had both immigrated here whilst quite young they nonetheless were insistent upon speaking with thick accents and putting on a facade of being genuine Italians; this, due to the insecurity of the fact that they were neither Italian or American in truth, and existed in the context of a cultural limbo which catalyzed for them a petty type of existential crisis.

They maintained a common tendency of immigrants to value money and nothing else whatsoever, which meant that by the time they retired they hadn't any hobbies whatsoever, save for their enjoyment of tennis. In the summer months this kept them out of the house frequently enough which was a breath of fresh air, as my wife and I both worked from home, but the winter months were akin to Dante's ninth layer and they did nothing but talk loudly and watch television at blaringly loud volumes. I began to develop a belief in mandatory euthanasia at this point in time.

It was in the midst of one such winter morning that I

ventured, uncommon as was the tendency for me, to do some grocery shopping. The grocery store which was quite close to my place of residence, and which was seldom very busy, had naturally just shut down due to an inability to renew their lease. This meant the necessity of my venturing to the next closest grocery store which belonged to a large chain in the region.

It is implausible as to how such a large place of business could be constructed with such a small parking lot, and likewise absurd that such a parking lot should be so busy on a Monday morning. After spending about 10 minutes in a murderous rampage and driving in circles I did eventually find a parking spot. Once inside the store I saw that there were no shopping baskets placed near the entrance, though I located them at the opposite end of the building. Nonsensical, but predictable I suppose.

The store was, of course, packed with human filth. I made my way through collecting the items on my shopping list as promptly as possible but it was very difficult to move with any considerable velocity given the amount of people, most of whom were elderly. Once people reach a certain age they lose all sense of themselves in the context of their surroundings. Generally speaking, this sharp decline in cognitive faculties occurs at the age of 60. It is all downhill from there. This isn't to say that there aren't pleasant elderly people but such is the exception rather than the rule.

As I did my best to maneuver through the grocery

store, while the song Jenny by Tommy Tutone seemed to be playing in a perpetual loop on the store audio system, I reflected upon the necessity of euthanasia for the old. It would solve a great many problems in the world. Shopping carts regularly cut my path off in a hurry, then proceeded to move at a snail's pace, driven by absent minded fools. These people were nothing but mutton awaiting their slaughter, I reflected. They were swine who should have met their slaughter long ago, and were now already in the midst of decay whilst still living, if such meaningless and cognitively disconnected existence could in fact be called living.

I employed the use of the self-checkout machine, which I have found the elderly to avoid at all costs lest they choose a convenient option for once in their life, and departed the store with that ridiculous song resonating in my mind. I sat in my car and was prompted, by what I am not entirely sure, to calculate the numbers of the song. $8+6+7+5+3+0+9=38$, which added together makes 11. There was an interesting number. It is the symbol of contending forces for the Kabbalist, the dueling heads of Thaumiel. The antithesis to any notion of mystic union with godhead, the number in question brought to mind the image of an entity with two heads which constantly gnawed at one another. Yet 11 was also the number of equilibrium and balance. I pondered the connection for a moment and then speedily left that parking lot for the gym located only several minutes away.

When I arrived at the gym parking lot the situation

was no better and it was full save for a neglected area toward the back of the lot, which seemed to serve the purpose of a dumping grounds, where I usually parked. Once inside the gym I saw that, unsurprisingly, it was filled with the elderly. Naturally this meant quite a bit of waiting to utilize the exercise machines that I required for my daily workout. It was absurd to me that one person could remain at a weight machine for so long. None of this did anything to soothe my homicidal imagination, which throughout the morning had been the only part of me capable of moving with rapid speed. Why did these decrepit old corpses waste their time exercising in a gym when they could be living out their later years doing anything they wanted with their abundance of free time? I suppose they were trying to extend their lifespan, and how selfish that was in the midst of an overpopulated world. Theirs was the pinnacle of egoism.

Of interest was that, and it was out of character for me, I neglected to bring my headphones into the gym and was subject to the fetid popular music that they blasted from their building-wide stereo. A song in which the chorus states, "We ain't ever getting older" (lest anyone speak proper English) inspired in me, despite myself, further malicious thoughts concerning the unnecessarily long lifespan of humans in this region of the world.

Eventually I finished my own exercise and drove home, only to find, naturally, my elderly in-laws sitting in the living room that adjoined the kitchen, watching television. They were obsessed with watching anything that depicted royalty and wealth; I suppose it was a form of escapism from the fact that their own monetary accumulation, despite being their sole interest, nonetheless established them as middle class. To make matters worse, as I sat in the dining room to get some writing done, one of them began to play with the filthy dog, which entailed them squeezing a ball which emitted a high pitched squeak, over and over. Thankfully headphones exist and I put on some music in my ears whilst I worked, though silence would have been preferable.

Later that evening, after a dinner with my in-laws in which few words of conversation were exchanged, my wife and I retired to our bedroom. She was engaged in her schoolwork and I layed in bed in a state of contemplation. Finally I made up my mind, closed my eyes, and drifted into a sinister place upon the inner planes of the collective human consciousness that I sometimes visit.

I made my way through the labyrinth of tunnels which comprise the underworld, the navigation of which is best directed by sympathetic thought unto one's intended destination lest one discover themselves lost and wandering amidst strange worlds with potentially hostile inhabitants. My sympathetic link in this instance was a peculiar temple which had been lost to humanity several thousands of years ago but which nonetheless retained its presence in the dark archetypal reaches of the collective human psyche.

I stepped out of the tunnel and into a desert. The sun was blazing and the sand hot. The old temple structure was a short walk from the vast mountain cavern that I had exited from and I was there in a short time. A freezing wind blew from within the gateway to the temple as I approached it, being in sharp contrast to the otherwise scorching environment. It felt refreshing, despite that it carried with it an air of death. I stepped beyond the black threshold and found myself standing within an ancient temple of Apep which was celebrated in the earliest days of Ancient Egypt, though eventually destroyed and eradicated from history altogether by that same civilization. The circumstances surrounding this are of great interest to the scholar of obscure ancient cults, but their telling would serve no great purpose in the present work.

What I will mention is that the ancient Cult of Apep was but a mask for the ever more ancient Cult of Yig, a primal serpent cult of extraterrestrial and non-human origin which grounded itself throughout various human cultures in an era of prehistory. Remnants of this ancient cult could still be observed today, particularly by those who share an interest in comparative religion and anthropology. The original practices have, for the most part, fallen out of use. The Cult of Apep was an ancient expression of the cult which had still, at that time, preserved a healthy semblance of the exceedingly ancient Cult of Yig.

The priesthood of Apep had been awaiting my arrival it seemed. In appearance they were all an approximation of one another; male and female were nude save for golden jewelry, and each of them were adorned with a face mask that covered them from the nose down to the neck. Their skin was of a bronze hue and their eyes were with a yellow glare. They never spoke but communicated silently through feelings. I had learned to communicate in this manner with them and other ancient inner contacts.

I explained to the high priestess and priest that an abomination had come to pass in my own time, wherein humans lived to too great and age and no measures had been taken to curb the global population. This would only amount to the destruction of the environment of the earth, and had created a situation which was rather unpleasant for all. The high priestess grabbed my wrist and walked me toward a side of the temple where a large obsidian mirror was placed. She positioned me before it and images gradually appeared in the mirror. I saw the emissaries of the Cult of Yig, a strange reptilian species which was not quite physical or astral, but something etheric and vaporous, as they traversed the galaxy and seeded their cultus unto the collective minds of many a species upon myriad planets which contained biological evolutionary systems.

The vision faded and I understood its purpose; the high priestess wanted to affirm to me that the Cult of Yig would perpetuate regardless. Perhaps they had misunderstood my intention, or else desired to affirm their own. I intonated a sense of insistence on the matter and proposed the creation of a mechanism which would fulfill the request that I had thus far implied to the priesthood. The high priestess nodded and we formed a circle together around the central altar, upon which burned a black flame. At the front of the altar the high priest and priestess entered a state of copulation as the entire congregation concentrated our efforts into constructing through them a peculiar disease. Throughout this process we conjured dark and vile emotional powers which lay dormant in an even more obscure region of the collective human consciousness.

At the point of completion, by which the high priest and priestess completed their act of copulation, we watched as from the womb of the priestess there emerged a black sphere which surged with a powerful electromagnetic current. She handed me the sphere and intuited the instructions for its use. I thanked her and the priesthood and made my departure by stepping into the black flame upon the altar.

Holding the black sphere, I drifted through the void of eternity until another flame appeared in the midst of the emptiness and I passed through this gateway, emerging on the other side into the outer space just beyond the earth. I positioned myself upon the surface of the moon so as to face the earth and allowed the black sphere to float out into the open space between the moon and earth. I watched as the sphere began to sizzle and crack, then split into billions upon billions of shards which accelerated into the earth and targeted the minds of each and every human. One final shard turned its course and penetrated my own mind. I allowed myself then to drift back to the earth and into my body, where I awoke to find that it was quite late and that my wife was already asleep.

I slept well that night, and it was from that time onwards, for awhile at least, that I turned my worldly pessimism from the tears of Schopenhauer to the laughter of Nietzsche.

Almost immediately the effects of the ritual were observed to have been a success. In the coming weeks an epidemic ensued whose effect was taken only upon the elderly. There was not a specific age affected, although the range was unanimously between 60-64 years of age. Those beyond that range, without exception for the entire human population, were rapidly stricken with immobility and decay, which led to the demise of a significant portion of the human populous. Similar symptoms were observed in those of the aforementioned age range, although the symptoms themselves took on a broad variety of forms. Doctors and scientists were puzzled and were slow to recognize an immediate correlation between the apparent diversity of illnesses which nonetheless shared a common origin.

What ensued was a fascinating ontological state across human civilization. For one thing, my trips to the grocery store, the gym, and many public places in general were much quieter. Political progress accelerated as did social justice, for what that is worth, although it wasn't of any great interest to me. Perhaps most significant was that most humans, having gained the assumption that they would meet their demise at a more or less set age, lived their lives differently. Gone was the vague notion of, barring some unforeseen accident of illness, living to an age anywhere from 70-90 on average. The retirement age was naturally lowered to 45 and social welfare ensured that a healthy pension was provided for all people once they reached this age, and on a global scale at that, for the youth of the world, no longer hindered by conservative walking corpses, were insistent upon a global government that acted in the service of the people. It could have been described as socialist, however it lacked the social censorship and restriction that earlier examples of socialism had employed in a totalitarian manner.

In time, my Nietzschean laughter began to turn toward a Cioran desire for sleep. At present I am nearing the ripe old age of 60 and I know that my demise is imminent. I for one look forward to it eagerly, look forward to rest, and am pleased with the knowledge that I will never develop into an unpleasant burden for this world, which I can depart from having made a genuinely benevolent impact which was born of a combination of rage, composure and ingenuity.

The Hunger

The following data was extracted from the nano-recording software of a biological subject N-138776903255 following its demise by feeding to the murder hunger of inmate M-462. It is presented as evidence to support the criminalization of what is referred to as the "knowledge hunger". Evidence in the following datum will suffice to convince that the "knowledge hunger", apart from being in a state of disuse by the vast majority of global citizens, is a dangerous phenomenon which is with the tendency to incite ideological criminality of the type which defers our biological specimens from their necessary purpose. The recommended course of action is termination of all library facilities and a reassessment as pertains to the ease of allowance for partial-technological implementation going forward. The account of the biological subject in question is as follows:

All throughout the cities of the planet was the constant reminder of the nature of this reality. It was to be forced into the cognition of all citizens of the planet. Were they to willfully acknowledge these principles it would amount to active contemplation. In instances where they passively observed the principles, they would seed developments and perpetuation in the subconscious mind.

The principles were as follows:
Everything is infinity.
Everything is collective.
Everything is individual.
Everything is contradictory.

Simple enough for any person to commit to memory, these four principles, or four truths as the more religiously inclined considered them, were a source of unlimited food for thought. More importantly, they were food for the Hunger.

Everything was food for the Hunger and every living thing was possessed by It. The obvious expressions of the Hunger included the pursuit of food and sex, as well as attention and acknowledgement, but also the pursuit of knowledge, wisdom and understanding. All things pursued were for the satisfaction of the Hunger.

The intelligent lifeforms of this planet, by which we infer those lifeforms that employ the faculty of reason, had long since rejected all notions of virtue and vice, good and evil, or any such dichotomies of morality. It was concluded on a collective scale that the universe was amoral and that any and all sense of morality was only ever invented as a crude means of establishing order; one which was inevitably always met with failure.

The need for some higher deity was accordingly done away with. In a universe which always was and always will be there is no need to acknowledge anything beyond infinity. All that remained of religious thought, and only amongst certain sects, was the Hunger. Most perceived the Hunger in a secular manner, rather passively in fact, and went about their business in feeding It. Those who consciously worshipped the Hunger did so in vain, for the Hunger cares not from whence it is fed, so long as it is satisfied. There is naturally no chance that the Hunger will cease to be fed, for the timeframe in question was designed to accommodate it by necessity, but the Hunger could not by necessity be satisfied until eternity itself had been devoured by It. Even then, it would have to blissfully devour Itself for the sake of complete satiation.

As for the intelligent lifeforms, their acceptance of the Hunger as the closest thing to a higher power made life immensely pleasurable. The necessity of menial labor was eventually abolished entirely with the onset of a fully technologically automated global civilization.

The sexual hunger was appeased primarily by machines. A great many of the intelligent lifeforms remained plugged into such machines at all times in a perpetual state of near-orgasm. Others preferred the pursuit of sexual selection with still others who had likewise elected against use of the perpetual-orgasm machines.

The food hunger was appeased simultaneously by the usage of self-replicating nanomachines which, once implanted, provided a perpetual source of nourishment which adaptogenically changed in accordance with each and every subtle desire. As with the sex hunger, there were those who hungered for the food-selection activity, that of stalking restaurant after restaurant in search of their ideal satisfaction. The one type did not commonly deal with the other in any event; where those who chose full automation remained in private quarters, those who chose partial automation roamed the outer world. Citizens of the planet were free to choose between these alternatives as the Hunger dictated.

As for myself, I had spent many years in full automation, which entailed my being plugged into a wonderfully pleasurable machine within my apartment which kept my hunger perpetually fulfilled at the slightest indication of agitation. Agitation. That was the real meaning in all of this, I reflected one day. What was hunger, or desire in general, but a form of agitation? Philosophical musings such as this were forbidden by law of course, and I would have to keep this thought to myself.

Punishment for deviation from the Will of the Hunger was severe. Although rapists and murderers had long since received their sentencing in the manner of being plugged into a virtual world wherein they were free to satisfy their hungers freely, they were likewise employed as the executioners for those who deviated from the laws of this civilization and were free to enact their desires upon those guilty of ideological crimes, which had become, in essence, the only genuine crime that existed.

Ideological crimes were undeniably rare of course. For most, it was enough to experience the fulfillment of their every desire at any and all times. Those few of us who were truly outcasts and desired above all to be free of desire were considered highly problematic and every effort was made to ensure that we were unable to conspire together, lest the utopia of the planet be overturned; as though any of us could have possibly been so ambitious. What we, or I suppose I, for I could not be sure of any other and had never communicated these thoughts, truly wanted was a release from this entire system. Death would be the ideal.

Yet even death was a complex matter in this world. Life-extension technologies were formulated so as to extend the lives of all citizens indefinitely. There was the odd chance that one could be arrested for ideological treason and subject to an imprisoned murderer that, being released from their virtual world, would be enraged and hungry for carnage, but the chance was equally possible that one could simply be subject to a rapist, and being kept in a state of perpetual prisoner to some sexual deviant was an altogether unpleasant prospect.

I decided instead to employ a particular form of The Hunger, being the hunger for knowledge. Few made use of this hunger but libraries nonetheless remained intact, albeit in seldom use. Following my transition from fully automated to partially automated existence, and having grown tired of pursuit of sexual desire and food amidst what amounted to be far too many options with an equally vast amount of competition, I ventured on an overcast day (was it always overcast? I am not entirely sure) to the library at the center of my city.

The library was in the form of an enormous building which featured immense stone columns at the facade. Previously it had served as the head of the Department of Education, I intuited from an etching above the large front doors. Some research demonstrated that such an organization once functioned to educate young people on matters pertaining to the world at large, but had since ceased to exist. Children were seldom born these days, and when they were it was the protocol to transfer them through a sequence of fully automated technologies which provided them with the necessary sustenance and desire-fulfillment.

I spent my subsequent weeks in the library, not bothering to leave it at all in fact. The only other person there was a female "librarian" who was hooked into a full-automation device of pleasure and nourishment, and who never said a word or made any indication of being aware of her surroundings. Not another person entered the library throughout the duration of my time there, unless they arrived and departed during my slumber upon one of the couches, but this is doubtful. I discovered much of the history of this planet and of the history of our species. Remarkable was that there had once been many religions, most of which involved suppressing the Hunger in order to achieve some imaginary state of perception, and all of which were outlawed in recent centuries. I perused countless volumes on this subject until coming upon a book which was at the pinnacle of heresy. I was honestly surprised to even find such a text here. The book was called "The Nature of Mind" and the premise of it was that, although the universe was in a state of perpetual vibration and agitation, it was possible to enter into a state of absolute stillness through which one could be liberated from the cycles of desire, which were stated to be nothing but a catalyst for sorrow and suffering. I had up to this point never discovered anything which made such absolute sense.

The book included within it a manual in which were found exercises by which one could gradually learn to enter a state of stillness. I considered taking the book back to my apartment in order to begin these practices, but decided that I was likely to already be in the safest possible location for these. So it was that I began my meditation practices each day, and with perseverance became quite adept at them.

Meditation did not completely eliminate my agitation but it did help me to abstain from engaging in it.

Instead, I learned to sit in silence and stillness, and to passively watch my desires and agitations as they arose and eventually subsided. This was remarkable for me. The final practice was called Mahasamadhi and involved entering a meditative state which would be endured unto the moment of death. It seemed a majestic opportunity, but there was the problem of the life-extension technology which I had been implanted with at a young age. I then decided that I may as well take my chances at arrest and murder, reasoning that if I was put in with a rapist I could simply murder them myself and continue on a murderous rampage until someone else did me in.

The next day I ventured into the city square and sat at the center of it in a meditative posture. It was only a few moments before an automated police machine identified me as an ideological criminal and I was promptly apprehended and taken straight to a type of courtroom, the knowledge of which I only had due to my reading about them in the library.

The room was small, no larger than my apartment unit; evidently not many people passed through this place. Not another biological lifeform was present, and instead there were only machines. One, I deduced, was the judge who sat at a podium front and center of the room. Like the other machines, the judge bore a deep black lens at the area where the head of one of my species would be; humans, I believe we were once called. The remainder of the machine bodies consisted solely of a large block of steel, within which were contained various appendages that could be produced or retracted as was necessary. I was seated to one side of judge and had a machine next to me, presumably my defense lawyer if I understood the process correctly, while at the other side of the judge was a prosecuting attorney. These two machines looked at me with their lifeless lenses, proceeded to approach one another with their lenses opposing one another, and approached the judge. They stared at one another for a brief moment and the police machine that had apprehended me earlier suddenly approached me with a wicked appendage designed for grasping and dragged me out of the courtroom, but not before injecting me with a syringe which immediately produced in me a sense of utmost pleasure, so that I was made to find the entire experience quite enjoyable.

Beyond the courtroom was an elevator which brought us to an upper floor. I was delivered into a room which was windowless and held within it the gruesome scene of a disheveled man ripping apart the corpse of another man. I was in luck, it would appear. The machine injected me once more, seemingly with the same serum, although I already felt quite content with the situation, and departed, locking the door behind it. The disheveled man paid me no heed at first, but after awhile appeared to have become bored with the ravaging of the corpse, and turned to face me with a glazed look over his eyes. He smiled in a cruel way, picked up a surgical blade without having to look down at it, and lunged toward me. At this instant I closed my eyes and entered into the meditative state which I had been training myself in. As my body was sliced apart by the ravenous lunatic I felt only joy and bliss at the prospect of departing this world in which I truthfully had no place. Everything gradually faded into a state of perfect emptiness and stillness which was free of hunger, desire and agitation in any form.

The Cities are Burning

My father and I are driving in a car. We cross a small bridge many times, and at one end of the bridge is some type of warehouse. At the front of the warehouse, above a black steel door, is a warm lamp. The atmosphere is with a dense fog. We exit the car and make our way into the warehouse. It is dark inside and there are many corridors.

I make my way onto a pier that stretches out into the ocean. I stand at the edge and, amidst the fog, see the monolithic silhouette of an ancient creature as it approaches the shore.

I am visiting the large indoor swimming pool and feel nervous at first about diving in. I am swimming and see that there are anthropomorphic animals around me.

One is a tiger who says something to me in a booming voice that I do not understand. I sink into the water.

Now I have found my way to the lost and fabled city which many have pondered but few have visited. It is a dark city and the stars shine a black light here. A dim green light is sometimes cast upon the myriad cobblestone alleyways, although the source of that light is unknown; the residents speculate about it sometimes but they are usually preoccupied with their agendas.

I move very fast through this city and every instance of time is as a flickering instant of fresh novelty. It is, however, always with a further revelation of seediness of the inhabitants of this place. They cannot help themselves, but they cannot be trusted, it is true.

My rapid movements take me to the outskirts of the city where there is a great open valley. The skeleton of a dragon lays in the valley and is suddenly animated. It speaks in a bellowing voice, "You will never leave this place." I am horrified and quickly make my escape away from the city and valley, to a place where I would never be suspected.

It is the time for my high school reunion; I had received my invitation in the mail. All of the young men of St. Peters are in the blue cafeteria seated together at a long table. There is no more room, but I find a young man alone at another table. In the past I bullied him, just as the others bullied me. I hope to make amends but he informs me that he will be going out for lunch today. I am seated alone now and decide that it may be better for me to leave as well.

As I descend the declining hallway some old acquaintances catch up to me. "We need to get a keg of beer", one of them informs me. We drive along Bay Street to an old neighborhood where the beer kegs are kept upon the high landing of a crumbling house. I see that I am expected to do the dirty work, so I muster the courage and make my ascent, being careful not to fall. Below they wait outside the car. I toss down a keg and we begin to drive toward oblivion.

My real estate agent informs me of a mansion for sale in New Jersey; it is located on a small island a little way from the shoreline. I recognize the mansion immediately; I have been there before.

My agent, my wife, three friends and myself arrive by helicopter to the mansion which comprises most of the island. It is a very foggy day and the sea is restless. At the facade of the mansion is an enormous brass dragon. We enter the mansion, with myself leading the way. I wonder if there is anyone here and the thought makes me nervous. The mansion is decadently furnished and decorated and there are many rooms, but it is also quite dark, save for a warm lantern in the kitchen which hangs over a red table, and candles in the study.

A crazed scrawny man approaches me aggressively in the study. I try to reason with him that we can talk, and endeavor to treat him as an equal, but he insists that he must come to possess my body. He grasps me so I take hold of him and bring him by force into a vast fire which I have conjured. His grasp is loosened by the flames and he burns up into nothingness.

The next morning I make my way to school but run into an old acquaintance along the way, whose name was the same as the lonely boy at the reunion. We must be careful, as a volcano has just erupted and the lava is still very hot. We cross a small bridge into a town in which not much has changed in a long time, and my acquaintance wants to visit the arcade. Inside, I see that there are many tiny lights upon the walls and ceiling, as well as red carpets and curtains.

I decide to take the back way to my school and meet others along the way, which is for the most part a wooded path. They are all very concerned about the dangers that lurk in the woods, the spiders specifically. I make my way to school from the front path instead. All of the students are walking in. I walk down to the locker room which is also the bathroom, and see that it is flooded with water. This has been an ongoing problem, I recall, and decide it best to leave the school. At my paternal grandmother's house all is not right. There is a mirror which reveals things truly horrifying, for it is a gateway to the other side. I am trapped here though, and everything is old and antiquated. I decide to enter the mirror and find after all that it was quite easy to pass through. Once on the other side I go to the garage and take their car, proceeding to drive around the housing development slowly. None of my friends are out and there are fissures in road which are best avoided.

I stop at the convenience store which feels somehow isolated from the world. There is an intriguing glowing green liquid for sale, but I do not purchase it. Instead I make my way up the mountain, careful to avoid the large spiders, and find that my uncle's house is in a sorry state. There is an acoustic guitar in his living room that I desire to play, but tarantulas surround it and I am frightened.

Once at the hotel I am reassured that I am very much welcome to the gathering. There are many people, most of whom I do not recognize. I ride the elevator but it doesn't open anywhere aside from the ground floor, so I venture out into the red desert. The cacti are not quite what they seem, but I do not mind this, and the sun is setting which casts a beautiful array of colors.

A strange entity is reading my cards. The first is Innocence and displays a man diving off of a cliff into alligator infested waters. The second is the Void and displays a whirling dark vortex. The third I cannot recall, but sense it will be revealed at a later time. All the while there are little creatures from another dimension residing in my reptile tank, and this gives me mixed feelings.

The city is burning and I am in the apartment of a girl

that I love. She is of medium height, blonde and lithe. The television is on but I pay no mind to it. The girl is sobbing but also laughing, and I feel a longing for her. The bus ride in Italy is with great confusion, for I was meant to take a train. A pretty girl shows me the correct path on a transit map and invites me to her apartment for a social gathering. I arrive later on and can sense that we have a mutual desire for one another. We begin to make love on the floor of the dining room and nobody else seems to notice. Suddenly we stop and I am left unsatisfied. I depart into the night and find that the sun rises very quickly, revealing that I have arrived at a rocky outpost that I have often frequented. One must be careful not to fall, for the depths are endless and the paths are narrow. It is worth it of course, for the sights are beautiful and just ahead is a place of luxurious fulfillment in the suspended city. My mother will be meeting me there, as will my aunt and sister. We will have to find a place to eat, which may not be easy as they are all quite busy at this hour.

Our stay at the resort has been wonderful. The common area is with stone columns that reach endlessly into the sky, and our suite is vast and open. I enter my room but quickly depart and go for a drive. Once I am a little way out of the area everything is swampy and somewhat dilapidated. I stop at an old gas station which is long abandoned and then continue onward, taking in the sights.

I am sorry to leave Florida but must return for now to the burning city. The apartment buildings are aflame and I feel entirely indifferent to this. Apparently so does everyone else, and the pedestrians walk about casually. Burning segments of buildings occasionally fall into the street, sometimes crushing cars and setting them aflame. Something about it begins to excite me a little. A change has been overdue after all.

The trains are very complex here but I have long mastered their navigation. Their pathways are like roller coasters and I find myself in a part of the city that is yet to be burning. It is not to my liking and for that matter neither are the security guards that stand along the office building. Their presence is a sign that I will not be welcome, so I take a return train to the carnival in Brooklyn and watch the pretty lights for awhile. Everything is abandoned here and only scrap yards remain. I walk for a long time and eventually reach a house with a nice, albeit small, kitchen, and eat breakfast with some relatives. There is a lovely vase of fresh flowers on the table and they emit a sweet scent. The back door is open and reveals a sunny green pasture.

Abdul Nakra has been a writer of strange fiction from about his 5th year of life, following a series of traumatic events which acted as a catalyst for the various creative pursuits that he would go on to engage in throughout the entirety of his life. Other creative endeavors of Abdul include noise art and painting. He considers himself a cosmicist philosopher, and also a cosmic pessimist. Abdul resides in New York City, a fact which he finds absolutely unfortunate. If you find that you must contact Abdul, he may be reached via email at SummonGobogeg@gmail.com.

Made in the USA
Columbia, SC
01 August 2021